Baby-sitters on Board!

THE BABY-SITTERS CLUB®

SUPER SPECIAL #1

Baby-sitters on Board!

ANN M. MARTIN

SCHOLASTIC INC.

*This book is for
Kate and Peter,
very special friends.*

Copyright © 1988 by Ann M. Martin

This book was originally published in paperback by Scholastic Inc. in 1988.

ISBN 978-1-338-81466-8

10 9 8 7 6 5 4 3 2 1   22 23 24 25 26

Printed in the U.S.A. 40
This edition first printing 2022

Book design by Maeve Norton

CHAPTER 1

Kristy

"We're here! We're actually here!" I cried. "I can't believe it!"

"Haven't you ever been in an airport before, Kristy?" asked my friend Dawn. Dawn Schafer has taken lots of plane trips.

"Of course I've been in an airport. But I've never been on a plane. Oh, I am so excited!"

"Kristy! Slow down," called my mother. She was standing at the entrance to the airport, struggling with suitcases and tote bags and plane tickets. "Don't get too far ahead. We have to stay together."

I slowed to a stop. At that moment, I would have done anything anyone told me to do. That was how grateful I was that I was finally going to get on a plane and take a trip — first a cruise through the Bahamas, and then on to Disney World for three wonderful days.

Mom and Dawn and I weren't the only ones going on the trip. If you can believe it, I was traveling with *twenty-one* other people — my entire family, my friends in the Baby-sitters Club, and all the Pikes.

This is what had happened: Mr. Pike, who is the father of a big family that the members of the Baby-sitters Club take care of pretty often, won a contest at the company he works for. Everyone was trying to name some new product. And the company picked the name Mr. Pike thought up. Guess what his prize was — an all-expenses-paid vacation for him and his whole family. The company booked them on a special group trip — a four-day cruise through the Bahama Islands and then three days at Disney World in Florida. But this is the really exciting part. Mrs. Pike called our club to ask if Mary Anne Spier and Stacey McGill would like to go along as mother's helpers. (There are eight Pike kids.) She asked Mary Anne and Stacey because they'd been mother's helpers when the Pikes took a two-week trip to the Jersey shore. When my stepfather, Watson, heard about that, and then found out that I had never ever been *anywhere* (except in western Connecticut, visiting my cousin Robin, which was no big deal since I live in Stoneybrook, in eastern

Connecticut), he did some quick planning. The next thing I knew my whole family — Mom, Watson, my big brothers Sam and Charlie, my younger brother David Michael, my little stepsister and stepbrother, Karen and Andrew, and I (Kristy Thomas) were going on the trip. And so were Claudia Kishi and Dawn Schafer, the remaining club members! They were going as our guests. Watson said he couldn't leave any members of the Baby-sitters Club behind.

The trip was truly a dream come true. A plane to Florida, then off on a cruise and three days at Disney World. . . . The Baby-sitters Club never had it so good.

"Now boarding at Gate Fifty-two — Flight Seven Twenty-eight. Repeat, Flight Seven Twenty-eight."

"That's us!" I cried. "Isn't that us, Mom? Watson?"

"Yes, yes. It's us, honey," my mother replied. "Does everyone have everything?"

"I think you should say, 'Does everyone have every*body*?' " spoke up David Michael. I laughed. I knew just what he meant.

Seated in a group of uncomfortable airport chairs were Mom, Watson, Sam and Charlie (they're seventeen and fifteen), seven-year-old David Michael, four-year-old Andrew, six-year-old Karen, and Dawn and Claudia. Nearby were the Pikes — eleven-year-old Mallory, the ten-year-old triplets (Adam, Byron, and Jordan), nine-year-old Vanessa, eight-year-old Nicky, seven-year-old Margo, and five-year-old Claire, plus Mr. and Mrs. Pike, and Stacey and Mary Anne.

I began to feel nervous. I hoped we could all stay together without too much trouble.

"Okay," said Watson, standing up. "Stay with me now, because I've got your plane tickets. Make sure you remember your knapsacks and cameras and purses."

I patted my knapsack. I could feel my camera inside. It was brand-new. Watson had bought it for me the week before. I couldn't wait to start using it. All my friends had brought their cameras along, too. None of us wanted to forget anything we saw.

"Tell me again where our suitcases went," said Andrew worriedly.

"We checked them," I told him. "Don't worry. Someone will put them on the plane for us. We'll get them after we land in Florida."

"Okay," said Andrew, but he still looked concerned.

I took Andrew and Karen by the hand then, and followed Watson to a woman in a uniform who checked the tickets, then smiled, and let us all walk by. We entered a long tunnel.

"Where *are* we?" I asked Dawn and Claudia. They were right behind me.

"We're in the walkway to the plane," Dawn replied. "I've been on dozens of these."

"It smells funny in here," said Karen, holding her nose. "Like coffee, only worse."

When we reached the plane, a flight attendant looked at the batch of tickets in Watson's hand again. Then we stepped inside.

"Hey, Andrew! David Michael! Karen! Look in there," I cried, pointing. "That's the cockpit."

"What's a crockpit?" asked Andrew.

"*Cock*pit," Karen told him witheringly. "It's where the pilot sits, right, Kristy?"

"It's where the pilot controls the plane," said David Michael. "See all those instruments?" he added importantly.

"Maybe," said the flight attendant to Andrew, Karen, and David Michael, "you could look around the cockpit and meet the pilot later."

"Really?" exclaimed David Michael.

The man nodded. "You might even earn your flying wings," he said mysteriously.

"But at the moment," said Watson, who was way ahead of us down an aisle of the plane, "you're holding up traffic. So come find your seats."

"Whoa," I said, as I took off after Watson and Mom. "I didn't know planes were this big. They look so skinny from the outside."

Rows of nine seats were arranged across the plane, with two aisles separating them. Two seats, five seats, then two more seats. Dawn and Claudia and I sat in the middle five seats with Sam and Charlie. It would have been more fun to sit with Stacey and Mary Anne, but they were busy with the Pikes.

I buckled my seat belt. Then I looked through the stuff in the pocket on the back of the seat in front of me. Emergency instructions, boring magazine, barf bag. . . . Ew!

"Hey!" I exclaimed a few minutes later. "We're moving!"

And suddenly the plane was in the air and the flight had begun.

"Hey, Kristy! Look!" David Michael, who was sitting behind me, poked something between my seat and Dawn's. "It's a barf bag!" he exclaimed gleefully.

"Oh, no. Look at *that*," said Claudia, pointing across the aisle. "Margo Pike is *using* hers. Ew, ew, ew."

"Poor Margo," added Dawn. "Stacey said she gets carsick. I guess she gets airsick, too."

Soon lunch was served. Karen and Andrew nearly became hysterical with excitement. "Look at all this great stuff!" Karen cried. "Salt packages, pepper packages, sugar packages, Handi-Towlettes. Even salad dressing! We better save everything, Andrew. You never know when we might need it."

"Take my stuff," I told her, handing my packets back to them.

"And mine," added Dawn, Claudia, Sam, and Charlie.

"Thanks!" said Karen. "But where are we going to put it all?"

"Put it in a barf bag," said Dawn. "That's what my brother Jeff always does."

After lunch, the flight attendant kept his promise. He took Karen, Andrew, David Michael, and three of the Pike kids (including Margo, who had recovered) up to the cockpit to look around.

7

While they were gone, I got an idea. I called to Mary Anne and Stacey. "Hey, can you guys come here? Just for a few minutes?"

Stacey looked around. Mallory and Vanessa were reading and the triplets were leaning over their seats, talking to their parents. "I guess so," she replied. "Everything seems to be under control."

Stacey and Mary Anne unbuckled their seat belts and walked unsteadily across the aisle.

"What's up?" Mary Anne asked me.

"I was just thinking. Since all five of us are on this trip, we should hold club meetings every day. Just short ones. You know, so we can keep track of what the kids are up to."

"Sure," agreed Claudia. "That's a good idea."

"One more thing," I went on. "It was awfully nice of Watson and Mom and the Pikes to take us on this trip — I mean, even if two of us are along as baby-sitters and sort of have to work for it."

"I'll say it was nice," said Dawn.

"So maybe we should think of something nice to do for them. Some special kind of thank-you. Maybe from *all* the kids on the trip."

"Yes," said Mary Anne. "Definitely."

"It has to be a *really good* idea," I said firmly.

"We'll think of something," Stacey assured me. "We've got a week to do it. Don't worry."

At that moment, Karen, Andrew, David Michael, and the Pikes returned. They walked proudly down the aisle with little gold pins in the shape of wings attached to their shirts.

"I think this means we're junior pilots now, Daddy," said Karen as she climbed back into her seat.

"That's very impressive," Watson replied seriously.

Mary Anne and Stacey went back to the Pike kids.

The flight continued. David Michael accidentally pressed his flight attendant call button three times. (The stewardess smiled the first two times, but by the third time she looked cross.) I took Karen to one of the tiny bathrooms at the back of the plane, which was an adventure for both of us. There was barely room for two people in it, and for the longest time we couldn't figure out how to lock the door. When we were ready to leave, we couldn't figure out how to *un*lock it. I nearly had a heart attack. I was never so relieved as when we got back to our seats.

At last the pilot announced that we would be landing in five minutes. I checked my seat belt six times. Karen squealed with excitement. Nicky Pike, who was sitting by a window, exclaimed, "Awesome!"

Margo Pike threw up.

When the plane landed, I turned to my friends. "We are here! We're in *Florida*! Oh, I am so, so excited!" I cried.

CHAPTER 2

Dawn

I'll tell you something. I have done a lot of traveling. When I was little, I lived on the West Coast and all my grandparents lived on the East Coast. Now my parents are divorced and I live in Connecticut with my mom and brother, but my dad still lives in California. All in all, I've flown back and forth across the country eleven times.

But I had never been on a cruise ship. In fact, I'd never even seen one, unless you counted the *Love Boat*, or the ship the Ricardos and Mertzes went to Europe on in an *I Love Lucy* show I once saw.

The *Ocean Princess* was bigger than anything I'd expected. Sure, the *Love Boat* looked big when it was photographed from the air, but I really was not prepared for the gigantic ship

I stood before with my friends and Kristy's family and the Pikes.

"Amazing," I murmured. I brushed my long hair back from my face so I could see better.

The *Ocean Princess* just seemed to go on and on and on. And up and up and up. I couldn't wait to get off the dock and on the ship. But crowds of people were trying to board it, and everyone had to wait their turn.

"It says here," said Mary Anne, who was standing next to me holding a pamphlet about the ship, "that there are swimming pools on board —"

"Pools?" I interrupted. "More than one?"

"Yup," replied Mary Anne. She was squinting in the bright sunlight. "Boy, I hope I don't get sunburned. Anyway, there are pools, a beauty parlor, a barbershop, a café, a disco, stores, and restaurants. Hey, there's even a health spa!"

"I don't believe it," I exclaimed. I was so impressed that I pulled my camera out of my purse and snapped two pictures of the docked ship.

The crowd inched forward. When we were halfway up the gangplank I turned around and looked behind me. A stream of excited passengers was waiting to board the ship. "I hope all these people are nice," I whispered to Kristy with a giggle, "because they're going on to Disney World with us. We have to live with them for a week!"

"More important," said Kristy, "you and Claudia and I are going to be sharing a room for a week."

"We'll be bunkies, like at camp," I said.

"I hope you don't mind a mess," said Kristy. "I'm not the neatest person in the world."

"No kidding," I replied. Kristy's locker at school was famous. It was one of the ones in which you might find a four-month-old lunch. Her room was always a wreck. And she never wore a dress if she could help it. Just jeans and sneakers and stuff.

"Really," said Kristy. "I hope it won't bother you, since you're kind of, um, neat."

"Spotless," I said quickly.

"Well, it's only for a week," said Kristy. "How bad can it be?"

"Right," I said. "We'll both have to do a little compromising, that's all."

A *little* compromising might have worked just fine . . . if our cabin hadn't been so tiny.

"It's — it's just like a hotel, isn't it?" I said brightly.

"A sort of a minuscule hotel," added Kristy.

"Yeah, I hope there's room for all my stuff," said Claudia. Claudia had brought along more suitcases than anyone else on the trip. She dumped them on a bed, opened them, and began hanging things up in the closet.

"Leave some room for us!" I exclaimed. I glanced at Kristy, but Kristy wasn't paying attention.

"This room is little, but it's cute," she said. "Two bunk beds, two dressers, a desk, four little chairs. Hey! Everything's bolted to the floor!"

"Oh, wow!" I cried. "I guess that's in case the ship starts rolling around. Gosh, look at all this great free stuff. They even left mints on our pillows!" I opened the door to the bathroom. "And in here is soap. Oh, and little bottles of shampoo."

"Look at this!" called Kristy. "Four new decks of playing cards — with the *Ocean Princess* on the backs."

Kristy removed the cellophane from around the cards and dropped it on the floor. I picked it up and threw it in a wastebasket.

Kristy changed her shirt and slung the dirty one over a chair. I folded it and placed it on Kristy's suitcase.

Kristy folded her arms across her chest. "Are you going to do this all week?" she asked me.

"Maybe," I replied.

Kristy crossed her eyes at me, and we both started laughing.

A low, booming sound filled the air.

"Hey, that's the ship's whistle!" I cried. "We're leaving! Let's go watch!"

"But I'm not unpacked yet," said Claudia.

"Forget it," I told her. "You don't want to miss this. Believe me."

We dashed out of our cabin and found Mary Anne, Stacey, Karen Brewer, and five of the Pikes in the narrow hallway. We all ran outside to the nearest deck railing.

A crowd stood on the dock below, waving to the people on the ship. "Good-bye! Good-bye!" we called, even though we didn't know anyone.

The people on the dock were waving and calling out things like "Bon voyage!" and "Have a great trip!" and "See you in a week!" One woman shouted, "Jimmy, don't you dare forget to change your underwear!" And another woman was silently waving a handkerchief. Tears glistened in her eyes.

Then someone behind me tossed out a

streamer, which unrolled as it went over the side of the ship. Someone else threw a handful of confetti. Then more and more until it was snowing little colored pieces of paper. It was noisy and confusing and exciting.

Slowly the boat pulled away from the dock. When the faces in the crowd grew so distant that they melted together, my friends and I returned to our cabins. But before Kristy and Claudia entered ours, I said, "Let's find out where everyone else's cabins are. I know we're all here in this hallway."

We began peeking in doorways. We found Kristy's brothers in the cabin on our right, and Watson, Karen, Andrew, and Kristy's mom in the cabin on our left. The Pikes, Mary Anne, and Stacey took up the four cabins next to Kristy's brothers.

"We've got almost the whole corridor to ourselves!" exclaimed Claudia. "Pretty cool."

"Well, let's go tidy up our cabin," I suggested brightly.

"*Now?*" replied Kristy. "What's wrong with it?"

"Girls, girls," Claudia jumped in. "Lighten up. This is our vacation, Dawn. We're not supposed to spend it cleaning. It's also only the first *day* of our vacation. I hope you two aren't going to argue for the rest of the week. It'll drive me crazy."

"You're right," said Kristy. "I'm sorry. But I don't like it when people pick up after me."

"I didn't mean to," I said. "I mean, I didn't mean to bug you. Listen, if you two don't mind, I'm going to go exploring." I turned around to check the number on our cabin door. Then I walked off. I hoped I'd be able to find my way back later without too much trouble. It would be awfully embarrassing to get lost and need someone to show me to Cabin P7.

I left the corridor, turned a couple of corners, and climbed a short flight of stairs. Then I pushed through a doorway, tripped, pitched forward, and ran directly into the most absolutely gorgeous, handsome, perfect, wonderful boy I have ever laid eyes on.

"Oh, I'm *sorry*! I'm so sorry," I exclaimed as we sorted ourselves out. "I wasn't look — I mean, I wasn't pay —"

"That's okay," said the boy, grinning.

His grin was as gorgeous and handsome and perfect and wonderful as the rest of him. Why aren't there guys like him at Stoneybrook Middle School? I wondered. The boy's eyes were a deep brown and they searched mine intently, as though, maybe, he could read my thoughts if he concentrated hard enough. His teeth, which I'd noticed when he smiled, were even except for a space between the top two middle ones. The space was cute. And his hair, which was the last thing I noticed (mostly because I felt as if my blue eyes were locked to his brown ones) was light brown and very straight — until the ends, where it curled into little tendrils.

"Some ship, huh?" said the boy.

"I'll say," I agreed. We'd reached one of the outside decks, and we leaned against the railing, gazing at the sparkling ocean.

"I can't believe all the great stuff that's on board."

"Me neither," I replied. The boy and I smiled at each other. "I'm traveling with my friends," I said. "A whole big group of us. Who are you traveling with?"

The boy didn't answer. He looked at his watch. "Oh, wow, I've really got to get going. I . . . I promised I'd come right back. See you." And he turned and strode away, leaving me alone at the railing.

What did I do wrong? I wondered. Was my

question *totally* boring? . . . And then I thought, I don't care if it was. That was the most gorgeous guy I've ever seen, and I'm not going to let him get away. At least, not this easily. This is a dream vacation, and I've just found my dream boy!

CHAPTER 3

Mary Anne

"Um, Vanessa, could you please hurry up? Just a little?" I asked patiently. Vanessa Pike is the slowest person I've ever met. Mrs. Pike once told me that she sometimes has to wake Vanessa twenty minutes before the rest of the Pike kids in order for her to get ready for school on time, and even so, she's usually the last kid out the door.

"I'm hurrying. Really I am," said Vanessa. "I just have to lace my sneakers up."

At least she's not talking in rhymes, I thought, which was what she did during the entire two weeks we spent in Sea City. (Vanessa wants to be a poet when she grows up.)

Vanessa slowly pulled the lace of one shoe through an eyelet. She stopped to untwist it, then pulled it through the next eyelet.

I glanced at Mallory, who was sharing a cabin with Vanessa and me. Without a word, we lunged for Vanessa. We each grabbed a foot and laced her sneakers for her. I didn't know what my friends or the rest of the Pikes were up to, but I wasn't about to spend half the day waiting for Vanessa to lace her shoes.

"Let's go see what everyone wants to do," I suggested. "Come on, you guys."

Vanessa and Mallory and I left our cabin. Next door was the cabin Stacey was sharing with Claire and Margo. Next door to *them* was the boys' cabin. The triplets and Nicky had been given a room to themselves. I had a feeling this wasn't a very safe arrangement, but it was the best one the Pikes could work out. Besides, the boys' room adjoined their parents', so how much trouble could they get into?

I knocked on the door to Stacey's cabin and then on the boys' door. The kids met in the hall.

"So what does everyone want to do?" I asked.

"Go exploring," said Nicky.

"Go swimming," said Claire.

"Go eat," said Byron, who's always hungry.

"Play video games," said Adam.

"Look at the ocean," said Mallory dreamily.

"Find a candy machine," said Margo.

"Read," said Vanessa.

"Look for people wearing goofy bathing caps and laugh at them," said Jordan.

"Well, I've got news," Stacey spoke up. "Your mom and dad said that you older ones — Mallory, Byron, Adam, and Jordan — don't have to stick with an adult. You can go off on your own as long as you behave yourselves."

"Awesome!" exclaimed the triplets, and they started to run off.

"Behaving yourselves," I called after them, "means no running and no laughing at people. Got it?"

The boys slowed down. "Got it," said Adam solemnly. Then he grinned devilishly at his brothers. They headed down the corridor.

Oh, brother, I thought. Please just let them stay out of *major* trouble.

Mallory asked to go off by herself, so Stacey and I decided to divide up the four remaining Pikes. Since the idea of exploring seemed kind of interesting, I chose Nicky. Then, "Vanessa?" I said. "You don't really want to read right now, do you? Come on and take a look at the ship."

"All right," she agreed.

Nicky, Vanessa, and I headed off in one direction, and Stacey, Margo, and Claire in another — in search of a candy machine and a swimming pool.

"Let's start on the very bottom deck and work our way up," I suggested. "We'll see what's on every deck."

"Great," said Vanessa and Nicky. And we did just that.

The bottom deck, which was called the Island Deck, turned out to be rather dull. "Just cabins," commented Nicky, sounding disappointed.

The next level, the Dolphin Deck, wasn't much better. Our cabins and the purser's office were there. That was all.

"What's a purser?" asked Nicky as we climbed the stairs to the third level.

"He's the officer in charge of money," I told him.

"Could I ask him for a loan? Just a couple of bucks?"

"I doubt it," I said, smiling.

The third level, the Providence Deck, was a bit better. We found more cabins, but we also found the ship's doctor, the infirmary, and a large restaurant called The Pirates' Den.

"Whoa," said Nicky, gazing around at the pirates' hats and swords and eyepatches that decorated the walls of the restaurant. "I hope we get to eat in here."

"But," said Vanessa warily as we passed the infirmary, "I hope we *don't* have to go in *there.*"

The Coastal Deck was where we found the Flamingo Cay Restaurant, the barbershop, and the Seven Seas Beauty Salon, as well as more cabins.

"Ooh, Mary Anne," said Vanessa, as we stepped inside the beauty salon. "Look, you can get your nails painted — even your *toe*nails!"

"Yeah," I replied vaguely. I was looking at a girl who was standing at the appointment desk, apparently waiting for someone to help her. She had masses of dark, wavy hair that cascaded over her shoulders and partway down her back, and she was wearing one of the skimpiest bikinis I'd ever seen. Even though she looked just a little older than me, she had a figure that filled out the top of the bikini nicely.

"Wow," I said softly. I was highly impressed.

The girl turned around then, and I blushed. I hoped she hadn't overheard me. That would have been too, too embarrassing.

But when she saw me, all she did was smile and say, "Honestly, traveling alone is such a *bore*. I have to do everything for myself — make hair appointments, talk to the purser. Have you ever traveled alone?"

I shook my head.

"Well, I don't recommend it," said the girl. "It's bad enough that my parents got ki —"

"Alexandra Carmody?" interrupted a young woman who had stepped up to the desk. "Lynnette is ready for you now."

"Oh, thank you," said Alexandra. She turned to me. "Excuse me. I've got to go. I have to get ready for my date tonight." Alexandra followed one of the hairdressers to a row of sinks.

I stared after her, openmouthed. What had she been about to say to me? That her parents had been *killed*? How horrible! Maybe that wasn't it at all, though. Maybe she was going to say . . . I couldn't think of another word that began with "ki" that made sense, though. Kicked? Kissed? Nah.

Imagine that. An orphan. Plus, she was *so* sophisticated. I could never, I decided, never in a million, billion years, be as sophisticated as Alexandra Carmody. Alexandra was even more sophisticated than Stacey or Claudia.

"Mary Anne?" Nicky was tugging at my hand. "Come on," he said. "This is boring. Let's go."

We continued our explorations. On the Tropical Deck we found a stage and theater for live productions, a casino with slot machines ("For adults only," I noted sadly), a room full of video games ("Awesome!" exclaimed both Vanessa and Nicky), a lounge, a pub, and a little restaurant called the Moonlight Café.

"This is my favorite deck so far," announced Vanessa, and I had to agree.

"I'm not going to say which is my favorite until we've seen them all," said Nicky wisely.

And after we'd toured the sixth level, the Moondance Deck, he said, "Well, *this* sure isn't my favorite." The Moondance Deck contained only luxury cabins, the children's recreation room, and a children's pool. "Baby stuff," Nicky scoffed as we passed the kids' areas.

But he perked up on the Starlight Deck, where we found another café, two fancy swimming pools, an ice cream parlor, a disco, a teen center, a bar, and — best of all — a movie theater.

"Presents ten movies a day," I read on the sign outside the theater. "Ten movies!" All thoughts of Alexandra Carmody flew out of my head. I *love* movies — old ones, new ones, love stories, space adventures, stories about kids in high school. "I'm changing my mind," I told Nicky and Vanessa. "I think the Starlight Deck is my favorite."

"It might be mine, too," said Nicky, "but look. We have at least one more deck to go." He pointed up a short flight of stairs, where an arrow indicated the way to the Sun Deck.

The Sun Deck, which turned out to be the very top deck of the ship, might not have been the most interesting level, but it certainly turned out to be the most exciting. At first it simply seemed, as Vanessa noted, "too healthy." It was where we found the largest of the swimming pools, a jogging track, lounge chairs, and the health spa.

"Boring," said Nicky, but just then Vanessa exclaimed, "Hey, look!"

"What?" I cried.

In a corner of the deck sat a shabby life raft. A tarp had been pulled over it.

"What's so great about an old raft?" asked Nicky.

"Not the raft, the head!" cried Vanessa.

Sure enough, a sandy-haired head was peeking out of the raft. A hand moved the tarp partway aside, the head poked even further up, and then in one swift movement, the tarp was shoved off, and a tall boy leaped out of his hiding place and darted down a flight of steps.

"After him!" cried Nicky.

Nicky and Vanessa chased the boy, and I chased Nicky and Vanessa. But the boy had gotten a headstart. By the time we reached the bottom of the staircase that he'd run down, he was nowhere in sight.

"Awesome!" exclaimed Nicky for the umpteenth time that day.

And Vanessa added, "I can't believe it. I cannot believe it! Do you know what, Mary Anne? There's a stowaway on the *Ocean Princess*!"

CHAPTER 4

Mallory

It was perfect, absolutely perfect. I couldn't have asked for a better arrangement. The thing is, I had just finished reading *Harriet the Spy*. Well, not really *just* finished, but pretty recently. I had finished it about a week before my family left on our trip. And I wanted to be just like Harriet. Well, not really *just* like her, since she had a lot of problems. But I wanted to keep a notebook like hers, a notebook in which I could write down things about people. And I couldn't imagine a better place to do that than on a huge ship full of people. There were bound to be some interesting ones to write about. Now, I know Harriet's notebook got her in trouble, but I wanted to keep one anyway. I'd just be extra careful that my notebook wasn't discovered the way Harriet's was. Besides, I'd be writing mostly about strangers, not about people I knew. I told myself that if Mom or any-one caught me, I could say that this was a writing exercise, which was true, and which would sound believable since I might become a writer one day. (You never know.)

The perfect part of the arrangement came when Stacey announced that us older Pikes — the triplets and me — were allowed to go off on our own. We didn't have to stick with Mom or Dad or Stacey or Mary Anne. Not that I don't like them, and not that Stacey and Mary Anne aren't a lot of fun, but it sure was going to be easier to spy and to write in my notebook if I could look around the ship alone.

So after the triplets ran off, with big plans to go find people wearing goofy bathing caps and laugh at them, I started to go off, too.

"Don't you want to come exploring with Nicky and Vanessa and me?" asked Mary Anne.

I did, I really did — but not as much as I wanted to go spying. "Thanks," I said, "but I'll look around by myself." I rolled my eyes, trying to make Mary Anne think I'd had it up to *here* with Vanessa, and Mary Anne grinned. Then I pretended to leave. I walked away, but after I'd rounded a corner, I hid behind a door until I'd seen Mary Anne go off in one direction with

Nicky and Vanessa, and Stacey go off in the other with Margo and Claire.

Then I ducked back into the cabin I was sharing with Vanessa and Mary Anne. I rummaged around in my suitcase until I found the new spying book I'd bought three days ago. It was a spiral notebook with a shiny green cover. As a precaution, I'd written OUR TRIP: A DAILY DIARY across the front. That was something that sounded fairly boring, should the book happen to fall into the wrong hands — not that I'd be careless enough to leave the diary where anyone might find it.

I grabbed a pen out of my purse and was ready to go, but where? The ship was huge. I'd seen a diagram of it showing where the shops and restaurants and swimming pools and everything were. There were eight decks on the ship, from the Island Deck on the bottom to the Sun Deck on the top. At least I wouldn't have to worry much about running into my brothers and sisters. If you wanted to, you could probably get lost on the *Ocean Princess*.

I decided to start my spying right where I was, on the Dolphin Deck, but all I found were cabins, cabins, and more cabins. No people. No interesting people anyway. Maybe I needed an interesting deck in order to find interesting people.

I made my way up to the Tropical Deck. That was the level with a theater, a casino, a video games room, and some restaurants and stuff. My luck up there was much better. Trying to look inconspicuous, I settled myself on a lounge chair on the veranda that wound around the deck. Almost the first person who walked toward me was a girl about Stacey and Mary Anne's age (or maybe a little older) with long, dark, wavy hair. She was wearing the teeniest bikini you can imagine, and she looked as sophisticated as if she'd just stepped out of a fancy penthouse apartment in New York City.

She paused to look at the ocean and soon a cute boy paused next to her. He smiled at her in this sort of coy way.

Gosh! Maybe something like that will happen to me someday.

"Great view," said the boy. "Look, you can still see land."

The girl yawned. "It is great, I guess. It's just that it's no big deal. I mean for me. I live down here."

Darn. So she wasn't a New Yorker after all.

"Well," the girl went on, "I live here when I'm not making movies."

"You're an *actress*?" said the boy. "Wow." He took the girl by her elbow and they sauntered off together.

I wrote furiously, trying to get down everything I'd heard. When I was finished the boy and girl were gone, but I stayed right where I was — like a fisherman who's caught a trout and decides he's found a lucky spot on the riverbank.

A few people strolled by me on the veranda — no one out of the ordinary. Then this old man came by. The thing that made me notice him was that he just looked so *sad*. He leaned against the railing and stared out at the water. I could tell he was thinking of something else, and that the something, whatever it was, made him feel just awful.

I was right in the middle of inventing a tragic past for the man when I caught sight of Kristy and Claudia. Oh, no! I didn't want *them* to see *me*, but it was too late to get up and hide. I scrunched myself against the back of the lounge chair and bent over as far as I could. At least they wouldn't be able to see my face.

Then they walked by and I could tell that, like

the man, they weren't really seeing the ocean, or anything else. They were very caught up in their conversation.

"I know I'm a slob," Kristy was saying, "but why should it matter to Dawn? Can't she ignore it?"

"I don't know," Claudia replied. "Why don't —"

"Excuse me," said a third voice, and I dared to look up.

The old man had stopped Kristy and Claudia! "Do you have the time?" he asked them.

"Sure," replied Kristy. "It's three forty-five."

"Thank you," said the man.

"You're welcome." Kristy smiled at him and she and Claudia walked on.

I left the veranda then. It might have been a good fishing hole, but I was too exposed there. I found a flight of stairs and walked up one level to the Moondance Deck. At first it didn't seem like much — just the children's recreation area and pool, and more cabins. But after I walked by a cabin with its door open, I realized that they weren't just any cabins, they were luxury cabins — huge. I decided to wander through those corridors for awhile. Maybe I'd see the sophisticated girl again. If she was a big-time actress she probably had a luxury cabin.

I didn't see her. What I did see was more interesting than the girl, more sad than the old man, and very curious. I turned a corner, and coming toward me down the hall was a woman pushing a little boy in an impossibly small wheelchair.

"We're almost there, Marc," she was saying. "Just wait'll you see our room."

"I *can't* wait, Mom!" exclaimed Marc, but I could tell he wasn't feeling as excited as he wanted his parents to think he was. I know because I've done that with my parents. Sometimes you have to protect parents and their feelings.

I stepped aside and sort of flattened myself against the wall to let them go by, but it wasn't necessary. The woman stopped when they were still a few yards away from me and entered one of the cabins.

"This is it!" she announced, steering Marc into the room.

I didn't hear Marc's reply. That was because I was too busy noticing, for the first time, who and what had been behind Marc and his mother. The first person was one of the ship's stewards, wheeling a huge oxygen tank. He was followed by another steward with a second tank. And *he* was followed by a well-dressed man

(Marc's father?) carrying a black box labeled: MEDICATION — REFRIGERATE. They all disappeared into the cabin with Marc and his mother, and the door closed behind them.

Wow. What was *that* all about?

I barely had time to scribble a few notes about Marc in my spying book before someone else came through the corridor, and when I saw him I nearly passed out.

The guy was about twenty years old with thick red hair. You know, that color that is *so* red you're just sure he was called Carrot-Top when he was little. He had flashing blue eyes, and when he grinned as he squeezed by, I could see that he was missing one of his bottom teeth.

Why did I almost faint? Because the guy was Spider from the Insects, my favorite group. I was *sure* of it. He's famous for that missing tooth. He lost it during a show when he hit himself in the mouth with his own electric guitar. I was just dying to ask him for his autograph, but I couldn't work up the nerve. What if he was one of those famous people who *hated* to be asked for his autograph? I watched him disappear.

Little did I know, there was even more excitement to come. I had barely recovered from my Spider-sighting when I stepped onto the deck (for some fresh air) and what should I see but a sandy-haired boy who climbed out of a huge pile of coiled rope, looked cautiously in all directions, and then ran through a corridor into the ship.

A stowaway! I wrote in my notebook. *I think there's a stowaway on board the* Ocean Princess. It was almost too much to take. What an afternoon I'd had — Spider, a stowaway, and all those other people. I decided to keep my notebook with me at all times, if possible. I'd have to figure out some ways to hide it in my clothing. This was going to be one exciting voyage and I didn't want to miss a thing.

CHAPTER 5

Karen

I love my big stepsister, Kristy. She is very, very fun. But here's one thing I don't love about her. Sometimes she doesn't believe the things I say. And just because I'm only six years old. I don't think that's fair. But it happens. Also, sometimes she says I'm too little to do things. I don't think that's fair, either. But it happens.

It was our first day on the big ship called the *Ocean Princess*. Andrew and I were really excited. We wanted to go swimming. We wanted to go exploring. And we wanted Kristy to go with us. But Kristy and her friend Claudia had gone off on a walk. Andrew and I hoped they would come back soon.

"Here they come! Here they come!" Andrew shouted a little while later.

I ran out into the corridor to see. Sure enough, there were Kristy and Claudia.

"Kristy!" I called. "Me and Andrew want to go swimming. Will you take us? Daddy and Elizabeth say they want to take naps after they finish unpacking." (Elizabeth is Kristy's mother, my stepmother.)

"Sure," said Kristy. "You don't mind, do you, Claud?"

Claudia shook her head. "Maybe I'll go look for Dawn."

"Are you mad at Dawn, Kristy?" I asked as she helped me change into my bathing suit.

"No. Why do you think that?"

"I just do. I can tell."

"Were you eavesdropping?" Kristy asked. Now she was helping Andrew with his suit.

"No, honest," I said.

Kristy gave me one of her I-don't-believe-you looks.

"Never mind," I told her. "Let's go."

Kristy changed into her suit, too, and then we were all ready.

"Let me just get David Michael," Kristy said, stopping by her brothers' cabin. "I bet he'll want to come with us."

He did. A few minutes later the four of us were way up on the Moondance Deck, standing at the edge of the children's pool. And that was when I remembered something important.

"Uh-oh," I said. "Kristy, I forgot my earplugs. I can't go swimming without them. I'm not allowed. I'll get an earache." Then I had a terrific idea. "Can I go get them myself, please? I know the way back to our cabin. Really I do."

"Oh, no," said Kristy. "You're not going alone. I'll have to go back with you. I mean, we all will."

"No way," said David Michael. "We just got here."

"Please let me go, Kristy," I said. *"Please?"*

Kristy scrunched up her face. "All right," she said at last. "You can go by yourself. But come right back, understand?"

"I understand! And I promise!" I cried. I dashed down one flight of stairs, then another. I knew I had two more flights to go before I reached my cabin, but I had to stop and look around the Coastal Deck. I *had* to. From where I was standing, I could see a big restaurant. Even better, I could see a beauty parlor.

I just love beauty parlors.

Sometimes my friend Hannie and I play

Beauty Parlor and fix our dolls' hair. We make them look very, very lovely.

This beauty parlor was called the Seven Seas. I peeked inside. A lady was having her nails painted. A big girl about Kristy's age was having her hair trimmed.

I forgot all about my promise to Kristy. I stepped up to the desk and stood on tiptoe. "Hello?" I said to the lady there.

"Yes?" she replied, smiling. She peered down at me.

I put on my most grown-up voice. "I would like to have my nails painted, please, madame," I said. "Just charge it to my cabin."

The lady opened her eyes wide. She looked a little surprised. "Just charge it?" she repeated.

I nodded. I know all about charging. Andrew and I have stayed in hotels lots of times with Daddy. Twice we stayed in a hotel in New York City, and another time in a hotel in Chicago. Whenever we're in hotels, Daddy hardly ever spends any money. He just says, "And charge it to our room, please." So I know you can do this. Except here on the *Ocean Princess*, I was guessing you were supposed to say "cabin" instead of "room."

The lady behind the counter leaned over a little further and peered at me closely. "Do you have permission to charge things to your cabin?" she asked. "Did your parents say you could?"

Daddy had not said anything about charging. Neither had Elizabeth. They hadn't said I could, they hadn't said I couldn't. But before I answered the question, I had to straighten the lady out about something.

"I'm not here with my parents," I told her. "I'm here with my Daddy and Elizabeth. Elizabeth is my stepmommy. Not my real mommy. My parents are divorced."

"Okay then," the lady said. "We'll need to talk to your father and stepmother. What's your room number, sweetie?" Se was checking a long computer list.

"It's P nine," I told her.

"P nine . . . P nine. Your daddy's name?"

"Watson Brewer."

"Right-o. Okay. If you'll wait just a moment, Judith will take care of you. She's the one over there," the lady said, pointing. "See her name tag? Why don't you sit down while you wait?"

I sat.

Soon Judith called, "Miss Brewer?"

I got to my feet feeling very grown-up.

Judith showed me bottles and bottles of nail polish and told me to choose a color.

It was hard to make up my mind. Finally I chose light purple.

"Splendid!" exclaimed Judith. "That will look divine."

And it did. But a manicure takes much longer than I thought it would. First Judith soaked my fingers, then she cleaned my nails, then she fussed with the skin around my nails, then she put on some clear stuff, then she put on the purple polish, then she put on more clear stuff, and *then* I had to wait for everything to dry.

"Now you be careful," Judith said to me when she finally let me go. "That polish isn't quite hard yet."

"I'll be careful," I promised. "Thanks, Judith."

While I was thanking Judith, the big girl who was having her hair trimmed was standing up and saying, "Thanks, Lynnette," to her hairdresser. She handed Lynnette some money. I guess she didn't know how to charge.

Lynnette glanced at the money. "Thanks. Let me get this changed for you."

"Oh, don't bother," said the girl. "Keep the change."

"But this is a hundred-dollar bill."

The girl waved her hand in the air. "Oh, it doesn't matter. My aunt is a countess. I have tons of money."

"Well . . . well, thank you," said Lynnette. She and I both watched the girl leave the beauty parlor. I was amazed. A countess — like a person in a fairy tale!

I remembered that I was supposed to be getting my earplugs, so I ran down to Cabin P9. I opened the door quietly and tiptoed in. Sure enough, Daddy and Elizabeth were taking naps. I found my earplugs and started up to the Moondance Deck. Halfway there, I decided I was thirsty. Very thirsty. I hadn't had anything to drink since I was on the plane.

Where could I get something to drink? I wondered. I didn't want water from a fountain. I wanted something more special. I climbed the stairs from deck to deck slowly. Each time I reached a new deck, I stopped to look around. And on the Tropical Deck I saw something called the Moonlight Café.

A café is an eating place! Daddy and Andrew and I ate at one in New York City. We sat at a little round table on the sidewalk. There was an umbrella over us. The pole went right through a hole in the middle of the table. Daddy said we could order whatever we wanted. I ordered crab's legs. But I didn't eat them.

The Moonlight Café didn't look anything like the café in New York, but I decided to try it anyway. I sat down at a table. The café was crowded. The waiter who came over seemed very busy.

He flipped open his order pad. "Yes?" he said. He didn't look at me.

"One Coke, please, sir," I told him. "And charge it to Cabin P nine. Watson Brewer."

"You got it."

The waiter brought my Coke. I drank it pretty fast. I realized I'd been gone an awfully long time for someone who was just supposed to be getting her earplugs.

As soon as I was finished, I ran upstairs to the Moondance Deck and found the swimming pool. Andrew and David Michael were in it, but Kristy was sitting nervously in a lounge chair.

"Karen Brewer!" she cried as soon as she saw me. "Where on Earth have you been? I was *worried*!" She got up and ran toward me.

I thought Kristy was mad at me, but when she reached me, she gave me a hug. "Don't ever do that again!" she said. (Her arms were still around me.) "I was about ready to get a search party going. Or call the Boat Police or something."

"The Boat Police! Are there really Boat Police?" I asked.

"No," said Kristy, pulling away from me. "Just kidding. But where were you? You better have a good story."

"We-ell," I said slowly. I hoped a manicure and a Coke were good stories, but I had a feeling they weren't. Kristy probably thought I'd gotten lost, or gotten into some kind of trouble. I couldn't lie to her, though. I held out my hands. I told her what I'd been doing. When I was finished, Kristy burst out laughing.

"You were getting a *mani*cure?!" she exclaimed. I nodded.

"How did you pay for it? And the Coke?"

"I charged them to our cabin."

Kristy shook her head. "You're too much," she said.

She gave me another hug. Then she got out her camera. "Hold out your hands again," she said. "Let me take a picture of you with your manicure."

I held out my hands and put on a great big grin, even though I am missing two teeth.

Kristy snapped my picture. Then she snapped pictures of Andrew and David Michael in the water.

I put on my earplugs and jumped in the pool. I am so, so glad that Kristy is my big sister.

CHAPTER 6

Claudia

I'll tell you something: I have never woken up on a ship before. It was kind of interesting going to sleep in my bunk last night. The ship was rocking back and forth very gently. I felt like I was falling asleep on a giant waterbed. And then this morning I woke up to feel the sway, sway, sway of the ship.

Except for our alarm clock, which rang at 7:30, I'd never have known it was morning, though. Our cabin is in the middle of the ship, so there's no window for the sun to shine through. And of course, since I wasn't at home, there were no shouts of, "Claudia, get a move on!" or "Mimi, I can't find my sweater!" There wasn't even the nice smell of coffee.

Nevertheless, as soon as the alarm went off, I sprang up. Luckily, I remembered just in time that I was on the top bunk. I lowered myself to the floor, stepping on Kristy's hand on the way down.

"Ow!" she cried.

"Sorry," I said, "but it's time to get up anyway. Hurry, you guys."

It was our second day on the *Ocean Princess*, and later in the morning, the ship was going to dock at New Providence Island in the Bahamas. We were going to spend one glorious day in the town of Nassau. I couldn't wait. Think of it. Me, Claudia Kishi, in the Bahamas. It was almost as good as saying I was in Hawaii, or on the shores of Tahiti. Tropical beaches, white sand, palm trees, cloudless blue skies, shells, maybe a cute guy. . . .

I woke up Dawn, who was sleeping in the bottom of the other bunk bed. (We were using the top of the bed for all the clothes I'd brought that I couldn't squeeze into our tiny closet or the dresser drawers.)

Then the three of us got dressed quickly, but silently. Well, *I* got dressed quickly. This was because while I'd been lying in my bunk the night before I'd planned exactly what I was going to wear. I put on my new blue-and-white bikini and over that, a pink sundress with spaghetti straps at the shoulders and big blue buttons down the front. Then I accessorized. I tied a pink-and-blue scarf around my waist, knotting it in the middle, added my snake bracelet and feather earrings, wound my hair up on top of my head, and finally put on these white sandals with long laces that you crisscross up your legs and tie in a bow.

When I was dressed, I sat at the desk and watched Dawn and Kristy. Dawn took off her nightgown, folded it, and placed it in a dresser drawer. Kristy slipped her pajamas off, leaving them in a puddle around her feet. Then she stared at Dawn, waiting for a reaction. After a moment, she stepped aside and Dawn whisked them off the floor and handed them to Kristy. "There," she said. "Are you satisfied? You wanted to make me mad and it worked, okay?"

"Oh, for heaven's sake, chill out, you guys," I told them. "Kristy, grow up."

Kristy stuck her tongue out at me.

That morning we ate breakfast at the Flamingo Cay Restaurant with Kristy's family. We sat at two tables — Kristy, Dawn, Karen, Andrew, David Michael, and me at one; Mr. and Mrs. Brewer, Sam, and Charlie at the other.

Breakfast at our table was just a little strained, but I forgot about our problems as soon as our orange juice was served. The waiter brought over a tray with six little glasses of juice, each one on a plate. My juice was the only one that was also on a napkin. When I lifted my glass, I saw that something was written on the napkin. It said, "I think you are beautiful." And it was signed, "A Secret Admirer."

"Kristy!" I yelped. "Dawn! Look!"

I showed them the napkin.

"Who could have written it?" asked Dawn.

"The waiter?" suggested Kristy.

"No way," I replied. (Our waiter was about eighty-seven years old.) Then I got a flash of inspiration. "You guys," I whispered, and everyone leaned forward, even the little kids. "You know who's on board the ship?

"Who?" they asked.

"Spider. You know, from the Insects. Mallory Pike told me so. She saw him yesterday with her own eyes."

"No!" cried Kristy and Dawn.

"Yes!" I said. "I forgot all about it until right now. What if this note's from Spider? A *rock* star. Wouldn't that be amazing?"

"It would be amazing, all right," agreed Kristy drily.

I made a face at her. Then I glanced at Dawn.

Dawn wasn't listening to our conversation anymore. Her eyes were glued to something across the room. I looked where she was looking and saw a Gorgeous Guy.

I nudged Kristy and pointed to Dawn. "Psst," I whispered. "I think Dawn's on the prowl!"

We started giggling and couldn't stop.

It turned out that I was right. Later that morning when the ship docked at Nassau, Dawn walked off like a zombie. "See you guys later," she said vaguely.

(Kristy's mom and stepfather had told Dawn and Kristy and me that we didn't have to stick with them. They said that Nassau wasn't *that* big a place, and we were old enough and responsible enough to go off on our own, as long as we returned to the *Ocean Princess* by five o'clock.)

No sweat.

The only thing was, Dawn the zombie had her eye on Mr. Gorgeous, and Kristy seemed to want to stay with her family. I could have stayed with them, too, but I knew this was the first vacation they'd taken since Kristy's mother had married Watson. So I felt that I should leave them alone and let them be a family.

"Well," I said brightly, as our feet touched solid ground again, "I'm going shopping. See you at five o'clock!"

I headed for the nearest store.

I just love to shop.

But I felt a little lonely and left out. I hadn't exactly expected to spend my first day on a tropical island alone. I guess I could have joined up with Stacey or Mary Anne and the Pikes, but I also hadn't expected to spend my first day on a tropical island baby-sitting.

I stood around in the store until I was sure Kristy and her family were gone. Then I stepped outside and took my first good look at Nassau. Little streets lined with shops twisted and turned in several directions. Palm trees and flowering plants were everywhere. The smell of the blossoms mingled with the salty air. I breathed in. Heavenly.

I wished I'd thought to bring a sketch pad with me. I could have made some terrific drawings of the beach and the people and the crowded streets. Oh, well. At least I had my camera. I could take lots of pictures to show Mimi, my grandmother. She's never been to the Bahamas.

I began walking and taking pictures, but after

three shots, I realized something odd was going on. Every time I looked through the viewfinder, especially if I turned around, searching for a shot behind me, I thought I saw a figure jump out of the way. The fourth time that happened, I glanced up to see who it was, but I couldn't tell. The streets were too crowded.

People in Nassau sure are polite, I thought. In Connecticut, they'd probably walk right in front of you and ruin the picture, not jump out of the way.

I walked until I came to a place called the straw market. Everywhere, local women were selling handmade straw crafts — mats and baskets and hats and bags. They were selling coral jewelry and embroidered linen, too; the most beautiful napkins and hand towels and pillowcases I'd ever seen. I know how to do embroidery — sort of — but not like this. Even Mary Anne would be impressed, I thought, and she does lots of needlework.

The crafts were spread out on tables or on cloths or mats on the ground. I kept stopping to examine things. Twice, when I knelt down to look at some baskets, a shadow fell over me. When I glanced up to see who was casting it, no one was around. When I looked back at the ground, the shadow was gone.

Weird, I thought.

I bought a straw bag for my mother, an embroidered glasses case for my sister, Janine, and a coral necklace for Mimi. Finding something to bring back for my dad would be more difficult, but I'd keep looking.

When I finished my shopping, I sat down on a bench to change the film in my camera. Then I decided to look at the gifts I'd bought. I pulled the straw bag out of my tote — and a note fell out.

I grabbed for it. "I still think you're beautiful," the note read. "Your Secret Admirer."

If I hadn't been sitting down, I would have had to find a seat fast. My knees went all weak. Where were my friends when I needed them? I was dying to show them note #2.

But I was on my own.

I looked at my watch. There were hours until 5:00. I decided to visit the Seafloor Aquarium.

The most interesting thing that happened there was that when I stepped up to pay the admission fee, the woman taking the money waved me through, saying, "Go on ahead, miss. The young gentleman paid your way."

My mouth dropped wide open. What young gentleman? I looked all around, but could only see some families and lots of little kids. I spent an hour at the aquarium, but I wasn't looking at fish; I was looking for my Secret Admirer.

Finally I gave up.

I went back to the little shops I passed when I'd first gotten off the *Ocean Princess*. It was time to buy a souvenir for myself. And to look for something for Dad again. I found the perfect thing (for me) in a jewelry store — a pair of mother-of-pearl earrings. But they were much, *much* too expensive.

"Sorry," I said sadly to the clerk when he told me the price. "I guess I, um, can't afford them. Thanks anyway."

I left the shop feeling sort of sad. I'd spent the day alone, I hadn't gotten a present for my father, I didn't know who my admirer was, and I couldn't afford the beautiful earrings.

I found an outdoor restaurant, sat down at a table, and ordered a Coke with an umbrella in it. When the Coke arrived it was served on a white china dish. The umbrella was in the Coke. A box was next to the dish.

I looked at the box and up at the waiter. He just shrugged. When he left, I opened the box.

Inside, on a bed of cotton, lay the mother-of-pearl earrings — and a note that read *From Your Secret Admirer.*

When I returned to the *Ocean Princess* that afternoon, my mind was whirling, and I felt dazed with excitement — and mystery.

CHAPTER 7

Stacey

What a day we all had! We compared notes that evening at our first official vacation meeting of the Baby-sitters Club. We held the meeting in the room Kristy, Dawn, and Claudia were sharing. (Mr. and Mrs. Pike had given Mary Anne and me two hours off, and we needed the break.)

Each of us had some sort of story to tell:

"Watson taught David Michael how to do the crawl," said Kristy. "David Michael's a terrible swimmer. He could only dog-paddle, but Watson took him to this really calm little bay, and you should see my brother swim now! I never knew Watson was such a good teacher."

"I spent the entire day with Vanessa and Nicky," said Mary Anne. "I was kind of hoping Mallory would join us, but she's been spending an awful lot of time by herself. . . . Have you gotten the feeling she's hiding something?" Mary Anne asked me.

I shook my head slowly. "Not Mallory. She's not a sneak."

"That's not what I mean," Mary Anne replied. "Not exactly. I mean . . . I don't know."

"Well," I said, "I'm surprised I'm not a prune. Talk about swimming, Kristy, *I* spent practically the whole day in the water with Vanessa and Margo. They are tireless. I don't know how mothers keep up with their kids. . . . What'd you do today, Dawn?"

Dawn lowered her eyes and looked shy, which was unlike her. "I sort of followed this cute boy around . . ." was all she'd say.

"That's a switch," said Claudia, "because a boy followed *me* all around today, only I don't even know whether he's cute." Claudia told us about her mysterious and elusive Secret Admirer.

When she was finished, Kristy asked, "Any club business?"

We were too keyed up to think of a single thing.

"What about presents for the Pikes and Watson and Mom?" she went on.

At first, nobody said a word.

Finally, Claudia suggested, "Candy?" just as Dawn said, "Flowers?"

"You guys are hopeless," Kristy told us. "This meeting is adjourned."

I looked at my watch. More than an hour was left of our two-hour break, and after my day spent baby-sitting and in the club meeting, all I wanted was to be alone for awhile. So Kristy went off with Mary Anne, Claudia went off with Dawn, and I went off by myself. I went all the way up to the Sun Deck. It was too late for sun, of course (besides I'd already had plenty of it that day), but I wanted to get close to the night sky and see the stars over the ocean. I'd seen a New York City night sky, a country Connecticut night sky, a New Jersey beach night sky, but never an out-in-the-middle-of-the-ocean night sky.

Apparently, a whole lot of other people had the same idea — even though there were really no stars to be seen. Sometime between leaving Nassau and ending our club meeting, the sky had clouded over and a wind had blown up.

I walked around the deck until I found a spot near the entrance to the swimming pool where no one else was standing. I stared out at the ocean swells, then up at the cloudy sky. I breathed in the salt air.

"Ahhh . . ." I said.

I didn't even realize I'd spoken out loud, but I must have because a small voice said, "It's nice, isn't it?"

I whirled around. Sitting behind me in the shadow of a doorway was a little boy in a wheelchair. (Mallory had said something about seeing a kid in a wheelchair. It was funny — she seemed to have noticed an awful lot about the people on the ship.)

Even though I'd wanted to be alone, I smiled and stepped over to the boy.

"It's beautiful," I said to the boy. "I just love the ocean."

"Me too."

"Would you like me to push you closer to the railing so you can see better?" I asked him.

The boy looked thoughtful. "I would," he replied finally. "I'll set the brake, but I'd love it if you could hold on to my chair, too."

"I don't mind," I replied.

I pushed the chair across the deck, and then he set the brake on the wheelchair. "Where are your parents?" I asked him.

"They're having a cup of coffee at the café. I said to them, 'Please, please, please can I go somewhere by myself?' so they said they would leave me here. I bet they'll be back in a minute, though. They really do worry about me all the time."

I smiled. I liked this kid.

"I'm Stacey McGill," I told him. "What's your name?"

"Marc Kubacki. I'm seven. How old are you?"

Seven? I thought. The kid *sounded* seven, but he looked younger.

"I'm thirteen," I told him.

"You want to know a secret?" Marc asked, craning his neck around and peering up at me.

"Sure. I love secrets."

"As much as the ocean?"

"More."

Marc grinned. "Okay. Here's the secret. I have a real bad heart problem. I'm not allowed to walk or run or do anything that strains my heart or makes me get out of breath."

"Wow," I replied. "What a drag." I paused, wondering whether to tell Marc about *me*. Not that he couldn't handle it. I just don't talk about it all that much. But the least I could do was be as straightforward as Marc. I drew in a breath. "Now I'll tell you a secret. I have diabetes. And my parents worry about *me* all the time, too."

Marc wanted to know what diabetes was, so I explained as simply as I could.

He nodded thoughtfully. Then he said, "This is our first big vacation. I wanted to go to the Magic Kingdom and Mom and Dad had never been on a cruise. So we decided to take this trip. I like the boat, but I can't *wait* for Disney World."

"Who's your favorite Disney character?" I asked.

"Goofy. Definitely Goofy. . . . Oh, here come my parents."

A young man and woman rushed over to Marc, looking concerned. But Marc saved things. "This is my new friend Stacey," he said. "She's holding on real tight."

The Kubackis laughed. We talked for a few minutes, and then I realized that my two hours were almost up. "I better go," I said. "But I hope I see you again soon, Marc."

"Okay," he replied. " 'Bye! And thanks for holding on! I hope your diabetes gets better."

So did I, but that's one thing about diabetes. You have it for life.

As I made my way down to our cabins, I thought that it really was a good thing I'd been holding on tightly to Marc's chair. The ship had started to pitch from side to side, and I was having trouble walking. I kept slamming into walls and doorways.

When I reached our cabin, Mary Anne stepped (actually, she fell) through the doorway of the cabin next door. "Oh, Stace, I'm glad you're back," she said, getting to her feet. "We're trying to settle everyone for the night. The crew is telling people to stay in their cabins — a big storm is coming!"

"No kidding. Wow!" I exclaimed.

"Yeah," said Mary Anne. "I've got Vanessa and Mallory in there," she nodded toward her cabin, "but Claire and Margo are kind of scared and they're in with Mr. and Mrs. Pike."

"Okay," I said. "Thanks."

I retrieved Claire and Margo (who did seem a little frightened, but not *too* scared), and tucked them into the bottom bunks in our cabin. I was trying to climb into my top bunk when the ship tipped way over on one side.

"Whoa!" I cried as I slipped back down to the floor.

A box of Kleenex flew over my head, and Claire's bathing suit sailed by.

"Boy, now I see why all the furniture is stuck to the floor," said Claire.

But Margo said, "Stacey! Stacey! I don't feel well."

Uh-oh, I thought. Margo is famous for her

motion sickness, and I can't stand to see people throw up.

I gave Margo a hug, though, and handed her a trash can. "Here," I said, "if you have to get sick, you can do it in there, okay? I'm going to run to your parents' cabin and see if it's okay to give you some Dramamine."

"Oh, don't leave," wailed Margo. But I had to. The Dramamine was in Mrs. Pike's suitcase.

"I'll stay with you, Margo," said Claire, looking worried.

I dashed to the Pikes' cabin, and Mrs. Pike returned with me, and then took Margo (who had thrown up twice in the wastebasket) back to her room for the night.

Then I had to clean out the wastebasket, which was really really really disgusting, but that was part of my job. Baby-sitting isn't always fun and games. Still, after I'd finished, the rest of the evening was kind of fun. There was no way Claire was going to go to sleep for awhile, so she and I watched things slide around. We took pictures of a suitcase that had dumped open, and of a banana flying through the air. (Well, I hope I got the banana.) I even took a picture of Claire laughing hysterically as she fell out of bed.

When she finally got tired, we lay together in her bunk and listened to the howling wind and lashing rain. At last Claire fell asleep and I climbed up to my bed.

The next morning, the sea was calm, the sky was clear, and the sun was shining.

CHAPTER 8

Kristy

The last thing I expected when I woke up on the morning of the third day of the cruise was a calm sea. The storm was over.

"I don't believe it," I said to Claudia as she climbed down from the top of our bunk. "I thought for sure — OW! Can't you get out of bed without stepping on me?"

"Sorry," said Claudia. "I'm just not used to this thing. People always talk about *climbing* into or out of bed, but I never thought of that in terms of ladders. It doesn't seem normal."

"Wake Dawn up, would you please, Claud? We're supposed to meet Mom and Watson and everyone for breakfast in half an hour."

Claudia had just stepped into the bathroom. I could hear water running. "I can't," she called. "You do it."

"Oh," I groaned.

"Never mind!" said Dawn. "I'm awake." She sat up quickly and hit her head on the springs of the top bunk. A pair of Claudia's shoes fell to the floor. Dawn frowned. "This room is a dump," she said.

"I don't think so," I retorted. And just to make her madder than she already was, I got up (without hitting *my* head) and swept two more pairs of Claudia's shoes off the bunk.

Thonk, thonk, thonk, thonk. They landed on the floor. I was doing it on purpose, and I knew it would make Dawn mad. It would serve her right for being such a neatnik.

Dawn stomped around, picked up all six shoes, and threw them back on the bed. Then she found the wrappers from two bags of M&Ms that Claudia and I had eaten the night before, and threw them into the trash can with such force that they almost bounced back out again.

I felt a little worried. Maybe I had gone too far with Dawn. Just in case, I decided to eat at Mom and Watson's table. And then I decided I needed to go someplace to cool off — literally. So I put on my bathing suit, grabbed a towel, my sunscreen, and this sports book I was reading, and headed for the big pool on the Sun Deck.

I wanted to go swimming, but it was too soon after breakfast. Watson says that that business about waiting an hour before you go in the water after you've eaten is an old wives' tale. But I'd eaten two poached eggs, two English muffins, and four pieces of bacon, and drunk both tea and orange juice at breakfast, so I was on the full side and decided to wait anyway.

I plunked down on a lounge chair, spread on my coconut-scented sunscreen, and opened my book. I hadn't read more than a page when someone else plunked down on the chair next to me. I hoped it wasn't Dawn. Unless she was coming to apologize.

When no one said anything, though, I dared to glance over at the chair. Sitting in it was an old man wearing a blue aloha shirt (kind of like one Stacey has) and green aloha shorts. The shirt and shorts absolutely didn't match. They looked awful together. Just as bad was the man's faded blue golf cap — and the look on his face. The look was so grouchy that I quickly turned my head back to my book.

But right away I had to glance at him again. Wasn't he the man who had stopped Claudia and me the other day to ask us the time? I couldn't be sure. There were so *many* people on board the

Ocean Princess. Besides, that man had seemed sad, not grouchy.

I turned back to my book. I read a chapter, then another. The sun was scorching. I decided it was time for a swim. I began swimming laps. When I surfaced after awhile, the man had gotten a glass of iced tea from somewhere. He tasted it and made a hideous face.

The next time I surfaced, I was just in time to hear the man say, "Clumsy fool." I wasn't positive why he was saying it, but a woman was walking away from him looking quite annoyed.

The *next* time I surfaced, the man had opened a book. But he wasn't reading it. He was looking over at a group of people who were laughing and talking and playing Trivial Pursuit. "No respect for someone who might want to read," grumbled the man as I hoisted myself out of the pool.

What did he expect? I thought. This is a pool, not a library.

As I was drying myself off, the man dropped his book. Without thinking about it, I leaned over and retrieved it. "Here you go," I said, handing it to him. And then I glanced at the title. "*The Mayor of Casterbridge!*" I exclaimed. "That's my nannie's favorite book. She reads it once a year."

"No kidding," said the man. "I've read it eight times. . . . Who's your nannie?"

"My grandmother. Mom's mother. She's seventy-three. She has a car named the Pink Clinker."

"No kidding," the man said again. "Seventy-three. Does that mean she's read the book seventy-three times?"

I shook my head. "Only fifty-eight. Once a year since she was fifteen. I guess I forgot to mention that part."

The man almost smiled then — but not quite.

"My Gertrude's favorite book was *Pride and Prejudice.*"

It was my turn. "Who's Gertrude?" I asked as I finished drying off and lay down on the lounge chair again.

"My wife. Dead now." The man turned away. His almost-smile had disappeared.

"I'm sorry," I told him. "Really I am. It's awful when people die . . . or go away. Nannie's husband — my grandfather — died. And my dad went away once and never came back. Now I have a stepfather."

"No kidding."

"Yeah. He's the one taking us on this trip. He's taking my mom, my three brothers, my two friends, my stepsister and stepbrother, and me."

"No kidding. Sounds like a mighty nice person."

"Oh, he is," I assured the man. "And generous. I think he'd do anything for our family. But you know what?" (Why was I confiding in this stranger?) "One of my friends that Watson brought along — her name is Dawn — well, she and I are sort of having a fight."

"No kidding."

"Yeah. I hate having fights. Especially when you're supposed to be having a good time. And especially when she's my guest."

"What are you fighting about?"

"We're kind of like the Odd Couple on TV."

"No kidding. Which one of you is the messy one?"

"Me." I looked down at my hands.

"Nothing to be ashamed of," said the man. "My Gertrude and I were like that. I was the messy one, too."

"Yeah? Then we're two of a kind."

"I guess," he replied. "Except that *you* look like you're having fun on this trip."

"Oh, I am," I agreed. "Not counting the problem with Dawn. Aren't you having fun?"

The man shrugged. "I don't fit in on this trip. I should never have come. I came for the wrong reasons. Besides, I'm too old and I'm a big grouch."

I giggled. "My name's Kristy Thomas," I told him. "What's yours?"

"Rudy Staples."

"Nice to meet you, Mr. Staples," I said, and shook his hand.

"Nice to meet *you*, Kristy Thomas."

Mr. Staples told me all about Gertrude then — how even though she was a neatnik, she'd been his lawn bowling partner, his golf partner, his life partner. But she'd had a heart attack and died just two months earlier. Mr. Staples had taken the trip for a change of pace. He said he needed to get away from his memories.

I didn't think the idea was working too well.

"You know what?" I said to Mr. Staples. "It's getting awfully hot out here. We don't want to get sunburned. Let's go inside. Do you know how to play Centipede?"

"That one of those noisy, beeping video games?" he asked with a scowl.

"Yes," I replied, undaunted. "Slobs like us love them. So come on down to the Tropical Deck. I'll show you how to play. I'll show you how to play Pac-Man and Donkey Kong, too."

To my surprise, Mr. Staples came along. To

my greater surprise, he was good at Centipede. When we were tired of the video room (Mr. Staples said his ears were ringing), we went back up to the Sun Deck. There Mr. Staples showed me how to play shuffleboard. To my surprise, *I* was good.

I looked at my watch after we'd finished a couple of games. "Gosh!" I exclaimed. "I have to go! It's almost lunchtime. This was really fun. Will I see you on Treasure Cay?" I asked. (That was where the *Ocean Princess* was going to dock for the afternoon, but you didn't have to visit the island if you didn't want to.)

"Maybe," said Mr. Staples. "Don't know what I'd do there, though."

"Just look around," I said. "See a new place. Treasure Cay is going to be almost like a deserted tropical island — I think. Anyway, even if it isn't, don't you just want to be able to say you've seen it?"

Mr. Staples' almost-smile returned. "Guess so," he said.

"Good. . . . Hey, I've got the perfect woman for you," I told him. "I mean, if you ever decide you want to start, you know, dating again."

"Who's that?"

"My nannie."

"No kidding."

"Listen, why don't you eat dinner with Mom and Watson tonight? I know they'd like to meet you. And you could meet the rest of my family, too."

"Well —"

"See you later!" I called. I ran off before Mr. Staples could say no. I ran all the way to our cabin. When I opened the door, I stopped and stared in horror. Someone had done something to the cabin while I was gone, and I knew who that someone was. Dawn. What she had done was straightened it up to within an inch of its life. Everything was folded up, hung up, put away, or thrown away.

Dawn had spent the morning committing a crime of tidiness.

I banged my way into Mom and Watson's cabin without even knocking. "Mo-om!" I cried. "Would you please talk to Dawn? She is driving me . . . CRAZY! No, better yet," I rushed on, "can I switch rooms? Can I stay in here? Karen could move in with Claudia and Dawn. Please?"

Mom was the only one in the cabin. She was sitting at the desk writing a postcard. "Honey, do you really think that's fair to anybody?" she asked.

"It's fair to me."

"What about to Claudia and Dawn? Do you think they want to share a room with a six-year-old? And what about Andrew? He depends on Karen."

"Are you saying no?"

"I'm saying I'd like you and Dawn to try to work out your differences."

"We can't," I said flatly. I left Mom's cabin in a huff.

At lunch, I spread the word that our daily meeting was canceled.

But I made Claudia spread the word to Dawn.

CHAPTER 9

Byron

Treasure.

I could feel it in my bones.

We were going to find buried treasure on Treasure Cay. All the signs pointed to it. I had just finished reading *Treasure Island*, and what was one of the movies they showed on the boat yesterday? You got it, *Treasure Island*. I made Adam and Jordan, my brothers (we're triplets), watch it with me. They didn't want to at first (because *Treasure Island*, the book, is a classic, and they think all classics are boring). But finally they came along.

On the other hand, our little brother Nicky and his friend David Michael *begged* to come with us, but we didn't want them. You can't keep people out of a movie theater, though, so they sat with us anyway. By the time the movie was over, we'd forgotten all about who did and didn't want to see it, and who did and didn't want to sit with whom. All we could talk about were pirates.

"A really good pirate," said Adam, "wears red-and-white striped stockings and has a black patch over one eye and a wooden leg."

"And a parrot that sits on his shoulder," added Nicky.

"And the parrot can squawk out, 'Yo ho ho and a bottle of rum,' " said David Michael.

"He wears one big gold earring," said Jordan. "The pirate, I mean, not the parrot."

"And he's rude and mean," I finished up. "He steals a treasure, buries it, and won't tell anyone where it's hidden. Except he tells his best friend —"

"Whose name is Old Bad John," said Nicky.

"— but he doesn't *really* tell him," I went on. "He gives him a hint in a treasure map. That's all. And he only does that when he's about to die. He figures that if Old Bad John is smart enough to figure out what the map means, then he deserves the treasure. But if he isn't smart enough, then the treasure should stay hidden."

"Right," said the others.

That was yesterday. Today we were still talking about pirates and treasures. And the *Ocean Princess* was going to dock at Treasure Cay! (*Cay*, which is pronounced either "kay" or "key," is just a word meaning *small island*. I asked my dad.) We were sure the cay was going to be like islands in movies — all jungly and wild with monkeys and coconuts and maybe a couple of pythons.

When we got off the ship, we sort of had a surprise. Treasure Cay didn't look too different from Nassau. I saw hotels all along the beach.

I glanced at my brothers and David Michael with raised eyebrows.

"They must have let us off at the wrong island," said Nicky.

"No way," I told him. "The captain knows what he's doing. They announced 'Treasure Cay' so this must be Treasure Cay. But wouldn't you know?"

"Wouldn't you know what?" asked Adam.

"There are thousands of cays and islands in the Bahamas. Only a few are inhabited, and we get one of them. Why couldn't we have gone to one of the other ones? It probably would have been real easy."

"How do you know all this stuff?" asked Jordan.

"I read a pamphlet," I told him. "Come on, you guys. Let's get going."

Since Treasure Cay was small, Mom and Dad had said that us triplets could be on our own, just like on the ship, as long as we behaved ourselves. The only thing was, Nicky and David Michael begged to come with us again. This time we didn't mind so much. They made up pirate stories that were almost as good as ours. But we had to do some fast talking to get permission. We got it, though, and so the five of us set off to explore.

"I don't see jungles anywhere," said David Michael, looking very disappointed. "Just hotels and swimming pools. Where are we going to look for buried treasure?"

"Where?" I replied. "Everywhere! Think, you guys. Were these hotels here hundreds of years ago?"

"Of course not," said Jordan. "So what?"

"So years and years ago, this island was probably just as wild as those uninhabited islands. A pirate could have buried his treasure here as well as anywhere else."

"Yeah," said Nicky slowly. "I bet lots of them did."

"Sure," I replied. "That's probably how the cay got its name."

"But everything must have been dug up when they built the hotels," said Adam.

"Not necessarily. Look at all this beach." I pointed up and down the sandy coast of the island. "They didn't dig here. And even if they did, that doesn't mean we can't be explorers."

"Adventurers!" added Nicky.

"Discoverers!" cried David Michael.

"Come on," said Adam. "Let's see what we can find."

Most of the people from the *Ocean Princess* had drifted away to try snorkeling or sailing or fishing, or to watch the shipbuilders I'd heard about. But my brothers and David Michael and I were happy on the beach. We peeled off our shorts and shirts and stood under a palm tree in our swimming trunks.

"This beach sure looks different from the one at Sea City," said Adam.

"Yeah, no waves," I replied with satisfaction. "Shallow water."

I hate swimming where the water is deep, especially when you can't see the bottom. But here, not only was the water shallow a long way out, but it was a sparkling clear aqua blue. You could stand in it and see your toenails and every grain of sand around your feet.

"Look!" cried Nicky. He'd waded out as far as his ankles. "Coral! I found coral!"

"Look at this shell!" said David Michael, joining him.

"Throw it back. It's pink," said Nicky, looking disgusted.

David Michael dropped the shell.

We waded through the water, following the coastline, until we came to a tide pool.

"Cool!" exclaimed Jordan. "Look at all those little animals."

We watched crabs scuttle along the bottom. They sent up puffs of sand. And a school of tiny silvery fish darted back and forth near the surface of the pool.

Then we walked to dry sand.

"Let's dig," I said suddenly.

"Huh?" asked the others.

"Let's just start digging. Right here. Right now. Maybe we'll find something. Look at that cliff of sand over there. Wouldn't that be a great place to hide a treasure chest?"

We all began searching. We turned over rocks, we combed through masses of shells, we dug deep holes in the sand, and we clawed at the cliff I'd seen.

Adam found a comb. Jordan found a pair of sunglasses with one lens missing. Nicky found a lobster claw. David Michael found another pink shell. (Nicky made him throw it back.)

But I was the one who found the treasure map.

It was under a rock, far back on the beach, in a spot where the sand would always be dry (unless it rained).

"Hey! Hey! . . . Hey!" I cried. I could hardly speak.

"What is it?" called Jordan, running over to me.

"It's — it's a treasure map!" I exclaimed. I held out the small yellowed piece of paper. "Look! There's a diagram and some funny words. They must be in another language. I wonder what language pirates spoke."

None of us knew. We tried to make sense out of the arrows and X's and lines that had been drawn on the piece of paper, but since we couldn't read the words, we couldn't figure out directions or where the ocean was or anything.

"Let's show it to that fisherman," I said, pointing down the beach to a man at the water's edge. "He probably lives here. Maybe he knows some stories about Treasure Cay."

But when we showed the map to the man, he just laughed gently and shook his head. Then he got a bite on his line, so we left him alone to reel in his fish.

Later, we saw Dawn Schafer walking down

the beach with some boy we didn't know. We showed the map to her, but she barely looked at it. She acted like she was in a daze.

"It's a *trea*sure map, Dawn," I told her urgently. But all she said was, "Mmm."

Disgusted, we let her and the boy walk on. It was almost five-thirty, and we were supposed to be back at the *Ocean Princess* by then, so I folded the treasure map and put it in my pocket. We headed for the ship.

"You know," I said to my brothers and David Michael on the way, "this map could be for anywhere. We don't really know. We could use it to look for treasure in lots of places. It doesn't have to be a map for treasure on Treasure Cay."

"Right!" cried Jordan. "We'll look everywhere. On the ship, at Disney World. Who knows?"

"Yeah," said Nicky, and his eyes lit up. "You know, there's a stowaway on the ship. Vanessa and I saw him. Maybe he has something to do with the map and the treasure!"

We all began talking at once. We had big plans.

CHAPTER 10

Dawn

"Ow!" cried Kristy. "Claudia, for gosh sakes, do you have to step on me *every* morning?"

"No," replied Claudia, sounding offended. "I don't. Not if *you* sleep on the top bunk. Then *you* can climb up and down the ladder."

"Nice try," said Kristy. "This is our last day on the ship. Tonight we'll be in a hotel. I have a feeling there won't be any bunk beds."

"Good," said Claudia.

"And wake up Dawn, will you? I wouldn't want to contaminate her or anything."

I smiled. This morning, Kristy couldn't bother me. Even the messy room couldn't bother me.

I was pretty sure I was in love.

Love is a tricky thing, so it's hard to tell, but there was no doubt that I felt different that morning. I felt a way I had *never* felt. It was a pleasant feeling. And since love is supposed to be both different and pleasant, *and* I had spent the afternoon before with the boy of my dreams, I assumed that I was in love.

It all made sense — in a confusing sort of way.

Even though I knew we were supposed to get up so we could meet Kristy's family for breakfast, I rolled over and closed my eyes. I wanted to try to remember everything that had happened the day before, on the most wonderful afternoon of my life.

Kristy and Claudia and I had gotten off the ship together. The three of us were going to spend the afternoon — at least the beginning of it — together, because we all wanted to try snorkeling. We'd heard about the water sports on Treasure Cay, and snorkeling sounded like the most fun. So when the ship docked, we immediately asked directions to the nearest snorkeling class.

When we found the place on the beach we also found a whole bunch of other people from the *Ocean Princess*. They were wandering around, trying on the masks and breathing tubes, and asking the instructor questions.

But I couldn't have cared less about masks or breathing tubes or questions. That was because

I'd spotted someone from the ship, and he was the only thing I could see, hear, or think about.

It was the Gorgeous Guy. Ever since the first time I'd seen him — that time when we'd actually spoken — we'd been eyeing each other, watching each other, smiling at each other. But that was it. However, when he saw me on the beach that afternoon, he came right over to me.

Kristy's jaw dropped. (Mine may have, too.)

"Hi," he said.

"Hi," I replied.

(What great conversationalists we were.)

"You here for the class?" he asked.

It was a dumb question, because why else would I be there? But all I said was, "Yup. You too?"

He nodded.

Claudia nudged Kristy then, and it occurred to me that I should introduce them to the boy, but I swear I couldn't even remember their names. (Plus, I didn't know his.) Claudia didn't care, though. She just smiled at me, nodded her head slightly as if to say "Go get 'im" or "Good luck," and walked away with Kristy.

"You know something?" said the boy. "I don't know if I *really* want to go snorkeling. This is probably the only time I'll ever be on this island. Why spend it underwater? That's no way to see it."

My heart sank. What was it about me? The boy and I had barely spoken two words and now he didn't even want to be in the same snorkeling class with me.

I had to look away. I couldn't let him see my disappointment.

But the next words out of his mouth were, "Do *you* really want to go snorkeling? Why don't we take a walk instead?"

I tried to remain calm. "Sure," I said. "That would be nice."

Nice? *Nice?* Couldn't I come up with a better word than that?

Apparently not. But the boy (what *was* his name?) didn't seem to notice.

We set off down the beach together. I knew Claudia was watching us and would be happy and not worry.

We walked down the beach for a long way. At first we didn't say much. We pointed out coral and shells and palm trees, and we gawked at the fancy hotels.

Finally I got up the nerve to say, "My name's Dawn Schafer. What's yours?"

The boy laughed. "I can't believe we haven't introduced ourselves yet. My name is Parker Harris."

"Parker Harris!" I couldn't help exclaiming. "That's some name. I mean, Parker is."

"It's a family name, my mother's maiden name. She didn't have any brothers — only sisters — so there was no one to carry on the name. Finally she just decided to call me Parker. It's not the same but . . . you know."

I smiled. "I think that's nice."

Parker reached for my hand. "You don't mind, do you?" he asked.

Mind? If we held hands? Was he crazy? That hand was attached to the most Gorgeous Guy ever to walk the sands of Treasure Cay.

We spent that afternoon just wandering around, enjoying being together. I barely remember what we did. Once, I know, we ran into the Pike triplets, Nicky, and David Michael. They tried to show us something, I think, but I couldn't tell you what it was. Parker and I were too busy being with each other.

The last thing Parker said to me as we boarded the ship was, "See you tomorrow, okay? It'll be our last day on the *Ocean Princess*. Maybe we could spend it together."

Another day with Parker? It seemed too good to be true. But he promised to meet me on the Sun Deck at 10:30. So after breakfast (during which Kristy strewed crumbs all over the table and purposely gave herself a milk mustache, which she wouldn't wipe off), I got into my bathing suit and went up to the Sun Deck. I was half afraid that Parker wouldn't show up, but he did, promptly at 10:30.

And our day began.

I had thought we were going to lounge around and go swimming, but Parker wanted to *do* things. With a mischievous grin, he said, "There's a Ping-Pong tournament today. Let's sign up."

"Ping-Pong!" I cried. "Only old people and little kids play that."

"Exactly," said Parker. "We'll give 'em a run for their money."

So we played Ping-Pong. I'd only played a few other times (the McGills have a Ping-Pong table in their basement), but Parker must have played a lot. Anyway, he was good. And we were a good team. We kept beating the other couples. I nearly died when Kristy and her old man friend took their turn playing against us, but I managed to psych Kristy out.

"Whoo-ee," I teased her. "Who's your boy-friend?" It was mean and I knew it, but Kristy had been mean to *me* on the ship. She'd been rude and messy and had made jokes about contaminating me. So I was glad to be able to psych her out.

Parker and I won the tournament. We were awarded a huge tin loving cup, which Parker said I could keep. After that, we ate lunch at the café and then we went back to the Sun Deck for a swim. We lay on the lounge chairs, drying off in the hot sunshine.

Somehow we started talking about divorce. I told him about my family. Then he told me about his. "You're lucky," he said. "At least your mom isn't remarried. I ended up living with my dad after the divorce and what did he go and do? He got married to this lady who has two little boys. They're five and eight. Right away, I asked to live with my mom instead. My parents said okay, but only for a month. I just moved back in with Dad a couple of weeks ago and he took me and my stepmother and the two brats on this trip so we could get to know each other better. What a stupid idea. I spend as little time with them as possible."

"How do you know the boys are brats then?" I asked him.

"Come on," said Parker. "All little kids are brats. Especially stepkids."

"I don't know," I said, trying to be patient. "My, um, friend Kristy" (I guessed I could still call her that) "just got a stepfather, a four-year-old stepbrother, and a six-year-old stepsister. And she loves them. Well, she loves the kids anyway. She's getting used to her stepfather."

"Remarriages are just plain bad ideas," said Parker flatly. "My mom's feelings are hurt, and my whole life has changed. Dad's being selfish."

It was hard to admit, even to myself, but I kind of thought Parker was the one who was being selfish. I didn't say so, though.

At that moment Parker suddenly jumped up and said, "Enough sitting around!" (I bet he meant enough talking about divorces and marriages.)

We went to the video arcade. We watched a movie in the theater. Finally, we found one of those booths where you can have your picture taken. I went in first and crossed my eyes and stuck out my tongue. Parker went in next and made monkey lips and flared out his nostrils. Then we squeezed in together and took two normal pictures of us smiling. We each kept one normal photo, Parker kept the goofy one of me, and I kept the goofy one of him.

What a wonderful day.

Parker and I decided to spend at least one day together at Disney World.

Was this love? Was Parker my first true boyfriend?

I decided that the answer to both questions was yes.

CHAPTER 11

Mary Anne

The triplets are in trouble.

Last night when they got back from Treasure Cay, they were all excited about something and they kept running through the ship. I didn't know then what they were doing, but whatever it was, they sure were noisy about it. They ran from deck to deck, thundering up and down stairs and occasionally knocking into people.

Finally one of the stewards caught up with them. He gave them a talking-to and led them back to their parents' cabin. The triplets stood by sheepishly while the steward spoke to Mr. and Mrs. Pike. When the man left, Mr. Pike called Stacey and me into the room. He explained what had happened.

"And so," he finished up, "the triplets are back in your care."

"Da-ad!" exclaimed Adam unhappily.

"Adam," Mr. Pike warned him. "You're in hot water already. Don't make it worse." He turned to Stacey and me. "At least for tomorrow," he said, "you'll have to watch all the kids except Mallory."

"Okay," said Stacey. "No problem."

"Right. We'll divide them up," I added.

We gathered the Pike kids in the cabin I was sharing with Vanessa the Slow and Mallory.

"Here's how we'll do things," Stacey told the kids. (She's better at taking charge than I am.) "Unless you all want to stay in one big group, Adam, Byron, and Jordan will go with Mary Anne, and Nicky, Vanessa, Claire, and Margo will stay with me. Mallory, you're on your own as usual."

Mallory smiled.

But Nicky jumped up and cried, "Just one change. Can I go with the triplets and Mary Anne? *Please?*"

The triplets looked at us eagerly — like they actually *wanted* Nicky to join them.

Stacey and I glanced at each other. I didn't mind being in charge of the four boys even though it would be a tougher job than taking care of Vanessa, Claire, and Margo. But what was this sudden friendship between Nicky and the triplets? Usually, the triplets can't stand Nicky.

We decided not to question it.

"Fine with me," I said.

"Fine with me," Stacey said.

My day with the boys began early. And we were quickly joined by David Michael Thomas. The five kids seemed to be in an enormous hurry and they were very excited about something.

"Just what are you guys up to?" I asked as I chased them up a flight of stairs. "And slow down. No running. That's how you got in trouble last night."

The boys halted at the top of the steps. Byron drew a rumpled piece of paper out of the pocket of his shorts. He glanced at the others. "Should we tell her?" he whispered.

"I guess so," Adam whispered back. Then, raising his voice, he said to me, "Promise you won't laugh. And promise you'll listen to us and believe us."

"I promise," I said.

"A fisherman laughed," Adam persisted, "and Dawn didn't even pay attention."

I didn't know what they were talking about, but I said, "I *pro*mise," as strongly as I could.

The boys told me about the treasure map. In all honesty, it was a little hard not to laugh. I mean, treasure hidden on an ocean liner? And a stowaway pirate? But I *have* heard of stranger things, so I held my laugh in.

"Well? What do you think?" asked Byron.

"I think," I replied seriously, "that there isn't much chance of finding a treasure or a stowaway on the *Ocean Princess* —"

The boys groaned.

"But," I went on, "it's true that you don't know what that map is for, so you might as well look around the ship."

"WHOOPEE!" cried the boys.

"*Quietly,*" I added.

"Whoopee," whispered Jordan, and everyone laughed.

"Okay, you guys," I said. "Lead the way — quietly."

The boys led the way. I followed them. When I got bored, I snapped a few pictures.

Click. I caught the five of them bent over their map, studying it.

Click. I caught Adam peeking under a tarpaulin.

Click. I caught Nicky and David Michael scaring themselves as they backed around the same corner from different directions.

Click, click, click, click.

After awhile, though, even picture-taking began to wear thin. I was bored. I looked at my watch. It was only quarter of eleven.

I sighed — loudly.

"What's the matter?"

I was sitting in an indoor lounge that looked like a hotel lobby. Around me, the boys were poking into things, peering behind potted plants, and calling out, "Hey, this would be a good hiding place for a stowaway," or, "I know! That arrow on the map must be the arrow that points down those stairs."

I looked up. Standing nearby was a beautiful girl — the one I'd seen in the Seven Seas Beauty Salon on our very first day aboard the *Ocean Princess.* She looked as lovely and as sophisticated as ever.

I was fascinated. There was the possibility that her parents had been killed. Plus, I knew that both Mallory and Karen had noticed her, too. Mallory had told me she was an actress and Karen had told me her aunt was a countess and she was loaded with money.

I tried to remember the girl's name. Alexandra?

"Oh," I replied, embarrassed. "Nothing's the

matter. Not really. I'm just a little bored. I'm baby-sitting for these boys and I've been following them around all morning."

"Yech," said Alexandra. "Children. . . . Haven't I seen you before?"

I was surprised she remembered. I mean, I just don't think I'm all that memorable. I nodded my head. "In the beauty salon the other day. You were waiting to get your hair done."

"Oh, yeah," said Alexandra. "Right. Honestly, that woman *butchered* my hair. You'd think that on a ship as luxurious as this one, they'd have a decent hairdresser."

"Gosh," I said, looking at her thick, wavy hair. "I think she did okay. Your hair looks great to me."

"Well, thanks," Alexandra answered, patting her head uncertainly. "My brother said it looks like someone took a hacksaw to it."

I laughed, but something about what Alexandra had just said didn't sound quite right. I couldn't think what was wrong about it, though.

Oh, well.

"Listen," I said, "my name's Mary Anne Spier."

"I'm Alexandra Carmody. But call me Alex."

"Okay, Alex," I said.

"So, what trip is this for you?" she asked.

"What trip?" I repeated blankly.

"Yeah. I've been on thirteen other cruises. This one's my fourteenth." (Maybe she'd gone with her aunt. Or when she was filming a movie.)

"Wow. This is only my first."

"Once we sailed all the way from New York to England."

"Gosh. . . . Who's 'we'? Your brother and you?"

"Oh, no. Just my, um, guardian."

"Oh." Alex looked pained, so I changed the subject. "Guess who is on this boat," I said dramatically.

"Who?"

"Spider."

"From the Insects?"

"Yup."

Alex frowned. "No, he isn't. I happen to know him really well. He's a good friend of mine."

I'd forgotten. She was an actress. Of course she'd know. How exciting to be in on the personal lives of famous people!

Suddenly I wanted to find out all about Alex. I decided to do something really daring. I hoped it wasn't mean. "So," I said, "how come you're traveling . . ."

Before the words were out of my mouth, I realized what was wrong with what Alex had said before. In the beauty parlor she'd said she was traveling alone. I was sure of it. But today she had mentioned her brother. If he'd seen her haircut, then he was on the *Ocean Princess*, too. And that meant Alex wasn't alone after all.

I quickly changed my question. "How come you aren't traveling with your parents?" (I had to know if they'd been killed. I just *had* to. I was dying of morbid curiosity.)

Alex hung her head. "My parents were — were killed. In a car accident. Six months ago. Now I'm an orphan."

"Oh!" I cried. I was horrified. "I'm so sorry. That's terrible."

"I know." Alex's eyes filled with tears. "You can't imagine how it feels."

"No," I replied. "Well, maybe I can. Just a little. See, my mom died when I was a baby. I never knew her. I guess I'm a half-orphan." The idea had just occurred to me. "I wish I *had* known her."

Alex looked at me sympathetically.

She was about to say something more when Jordan ran to me breathlessly.

"Mary Anne, we've tried everything and we've looked everywhere," he complained. "We haven't found a thing."

"I better go," Alex said quickly. "You look busy."

I tried to say good-bye to her and listen to Jordan at the same time.

"And we have four levels to go and the boat's going to dock in Port Canaveral," he continued, sounding whiny. "And then the cruise will be *over*."

"But we can still search for treasure at Disney World!" exclaimed Nicky.

"Yeah!" cried the others, brightening.

Their smiles returned, but mine didn't. I felt very thoughtful. I couldn't stop thinking about Alex. I felt really sorry for her, but I also felt close to her. You don't know how it feels to lose a parent or to grow up without one unless it has actually happened to you.

I knew I had found a true friend.

I just couldn't figure out why she had lied to me about traveling alone.

CHAPTER 12

Stacey

My day with the Pike girls began a little differently than Mary Anne's day with the Pike boys. The Pike boys knew exactly what they wanted to do. So did the Pike girls. Only they didn't want to do the same things.

Claire and Margo wanted to go to the stores, the children's pool, and the video arcade, in that order. Vanessa wanted to read. Period. She was reading *Baby Island*, and she was two-thirds of the way through and wanted to sit up on the Sun Deck all morning so she could finish it before the boat docked in Port Canaveral.

A fight was brewing.

"I want to play Centipede!" Claire cried.

"Sun Deck!" Vanessa replied loudly.

"Donkey Kong! Shopping!" said Margo.

"Reading!" shouted Vanessa.

"Girls, girls, girls," I interrupted. "Now hold on and let me think. There must be some way to solve this." (And I thought I was going to have an easy day, with the boys out of my hair.)

"I can help you solve it," spoke up Mallory. She was standing in the doorway to our cabin. "I want to go to the Sun Deck to read, too," she said, and I noticed the copy of *The Princess and the Goblin* in her hand. "Why don't I just take Vanessa with me? I don't mind watching her."

Vanessa looked at me hopefully.

"If your parents say it's okay, that would be great," I told the girls. I knew Mallory was capable of watching Vanessa. She's very responsible.

So we got the Pikes' permission, and the two happy bookworms headed for the Sun Deck. Then I took Claire and Margo by the hands and the three of us headed for the stores.

"What is it you want to buy?" I asked them.

"Gum," said Margo.

"A sewer-ear," said Claire.

"A sewer-ear?" I repeated.

"She means a *souvenir,*" said Margo witheringly.

We made a tour of the shops. Margo got her gum, and Claire bought a gaudy pencil that said "Ocean Princess" on it. Then they took a dip in the pool, as planned, and finally, dried off and refreshed, they set out for the video arcade. I followed, carrying their towels, the gum, the pencil, and five dollars from Mrs. Pike that she had said we could change into quarters for the games. I wondered what Marc Kubacki was up to just then.

And believe it or not, halfway between the stores and the video arcade, we ran into Marc and his father.

"Hi, Marc!" I said.

"Hi, Stacey."

At the exchange of hellos, Claire and Margo halted and turned around. They stared at Marc and his wheelchair, and then came back to us, looking curious.

Please, I begged them silently, don't say anything embarrassing.

"Where are you off to?" I asked the Kubackis.

"We're just taking a walk," said Marc.

Claire had stepped all the way up to the wheelchair and was standing directly in front of Marc. "We're going to the video arcade," she told him.

"The video arcade?" Marc repeated. He gave his father a pointed look, but I wasn't sure what the look meant.

There was a moment of strained silence. I broke it by saying, "I guess you guys don't know each other. Claire and Margo, this is Marc Kubacki and his father. I met them a couple of days ago. And this is Claire Pike," I went on, touching Claire on the head, "and Margo Pike."

Everyone said hi and I tried to explain to the girls how I knew Marc, and to Marc why I was with the Pikes.

Claire showed Marc her new pencil.

"Awesome!" said Marc.

Claire grinned. "How old are you?"

"Seven," Marc replied.

"*My* age!" exclaimed Margo. "You're *seven*?"

"I'm a little small."

"Not smaller than me," said Claire defensively. "I'm five," she added.

"Do you like video games?" Margo asked Marc, and I knew she wanted to get going.

"Yes, I do," he answered, giving his father that look again.

Mr. Kubacki shrugged. "That video arcade is so *noisy*," he said to me. "I'd do almost anything for Marc, but ten minutes in one of those places drives me crazy."

"Want to come with us, Marc?" asked Claire.

I glanced at Mr. Kubacki, remembering how protective he was of his son.

"I don't know. . . ." said Marc's father.

At least he hadn't said no. Marc began to look hopeful. "Could I?" he asked, looking from his father to me.

"It's fine with me," I told Mr. Kubacki. "We'd be glad to have Marc along."

"That way you could go take your swim," Marc said to his father.

"Well," replied Mr. Kubacki, "all right. I'm sure you're responsible." He was probably thinking about my diabetes, and my diet, and my insulin shots, which we had talked about the night I met the Kubackis.

"Yay!" cried Marc. "Thanks, Dad."

We made arrangements for where and when to meet, and Mr. Kubacki gave me a few quick instructions. Then we separated. The girls pushed Marc's wheelchair toward the arcade and I walked behind them. A few seconds later, I glanced back. Mr. Kubacki was watching us worriedly. I waved to let him know that everything would be all right. He smiled and set off for the Sun Deck.

"So how come you have to ride in this wheelchair, anyway?" asked Margo.

I cringed. But Marc replied cheerfully, "I've got a bad heart."

"Can you walk?" asked Claire.

"Of course," said Marc, sounding insulted. "But I'm not supposed to. It makes my heart muscles work too hard. I can't do anything that's like exercise."

"But you can play video games, right?" said Margo.

"Sure — if I can sit up high enough."

Oops. That hadn't occurred to me. How was Marc going to reach the game controls from his sitting position? But we solved that problem as soon as we reached the arcade and got our quarters. One of the ship's stewards was nice enough to give Marc two big cushions to sit on. Then he even gave Marc, Claire, and Margo each a free game.

The kids' friendship was cemented.

They were so awed by the free games that all they could do was exclaim over their good luck. Then they started talking about Disney World and the rides.

"I can't wait to see the castle!" cried Margo.

"Oh, Margo-silly-billy-goo-goo —" Claire began, and Marc burst out laughing.

"Silly-billy-goo-goo!" he repeated.

Claire and Margo got the giggles.

When they calmed down, the three of them finally played some games. But in between, their conversation continued. I was just thinking that the girls seemed done commenting about Marc using a wheelchair, when Claire finished a game of Donkey Kong and ran to Marc urgently.

"How are you going to go on Space Mountain in your wheelchair?" she wanted to know. (Space Mountain is supposed to be the wildest ride at Disney World. It's a high-speed roller coaster through dark tunnels that look like outer space.)

"Oh, I can't go on Space Mountain," said Marc soberly. "I can get out of my wheelchair to go on quiet rides, but not on a roller coaster."

The three kids grew silent. It was as if the girls hadn't realized how sick Marc was until he said he couldn't go on Space Mountain.

They were about out of quarters then and we weren't going to meet Marc's father for another half an hour, so I made a suggestion. I hoped it would perk them up. "How about getting a treat at the ice-cream parlor?" I asked.

This was met with cheers, so with the girls pushing Marc, we made our way to the Scooper-Duper Ice-Cream Parlor. It looked like an old-fashioned soda shop with little round tables and wire chairs with curlicues all over them. The waiters and waitresses were wearing red-and-white striped jackets.

"Hey, there's Claudia!" exclaimed Margo as we were looking for a table.

Claudia was sitting by herself, nursing a butterscotch sundae. She's a junk-food addict and looked as if she were in seventh heaven.

"Hi, you guys," she said.

"Hi," Claire and Margo and I replied.

Then I introduced Marc to Claudia.

"What are you eating?" Claire asked Claudia.

"A butterscotch sundae," she replied.

Claire made a face. "I want a chocolate soda," she told me.

"Me too," said Margo and Marc.

We sat at Claudia's table and ordered chocolate sodas. (I had to get a Diet Coke, which is one of the worst things about having diabetes — missing out on treats.)

When it was almost time to meet Mr. Kubacki, I took our bill up to the line at the cash register. I began to daydream but woke up when I heard the boy in front of me say to the cashier in a whisper, "And I'll pay for *her* sundae, too." The boy pointed across the room.

Why was he whispering? And who was he pointing to? I turned to look. He was pointing at Claudia! Or at least I thought he was. An older woman was at a table in front of ours, and a girl my age was at a table in back of ours. But neither of them looked like she deserved a Secret Admirer. He must mean Claudia. This boy must be her Secret Admirer!

I waved frantically to Claudia, but she was helping Marc with something. "Claud!" I called.

"AHEM! Miss?"

I turned back to the cashier, who looked very impatient.

And I realized that the boy was gone.

Darn! I hadn't even gotten a good look at him. But there was nothing I could do now. The cashier and everyone on line were waiting for me to pay.

I paid.

Then I flew back to our table.

"Claudia! Claudia!" I cried. "I think I just saw your Secret Admirer!" I told her what had happened and tried to remember what he had looked like, but I really hadn't noticed. "I guess you missed him again," I said sadly.

"Not necessarily!" exclaimed Claudia. "See you guys later."

It was her turn to fly. .

"Boy," said Marc, "this is the most fun I've had on the whole trip. You guys sure do exciting things."

He and the Pike girls smiled chocolate-soda smiles at one another. There's nothing like new friends.

I only wished that Claudia could find *her* new friend — whoever he was. But I wasn't holding out much hope. He was always around, yet he always kept himself hidden. However, Marc was right. It *had* been an exciting morning. I couldn't wait to talk to Claudia later.

CHAPTER 13

Claudia

I simply couldn't believe what Stacey had just said. Not the part about my Secret Admirer. I already knew I had one. What I couldn't believe was that Stacey had been standing right next to him, and all she could say about his looks was that she thought he had brown hair.

There was nothing to do but leave the Scooper-Duper right then and hope to see a brown-haired boy nearby. For a moment, I looked longingly at the five mouthfuls of melted ice cream that were still left in my dish. Then I jumped up and ran into the hallway. At least I didn't have to waste time paying my bill. My Secret Admirer had taken care of that for me.

I felt like someone in a spy novel. I burst through the doorway of the ice-cream parlor, skidded to a stop in the hallway, and looked left and right. To the left was a dead end. I took off in the other direction — and almost smacked into a boy who stepped out from behind a pillar.

He had blond hair.

"Whoa!" he said, and I tried to catch my breath. "What's going on?"

"Did you see a brown-haired boy come out of here a couple of minutes ago?" I gasped.

"Was he running like you?"

"I don't know. He might have been. Did someone run by?"

"Yeah, at full speed. He came out of the ice-cream parlor."

"Oh, please. What did he look like?" I asked.

"Hmm. Red hair, I think. Great sneakers. I really wasn't paying attention."

Great *sneakers*? What was wrong with everybody? Why couldn't they be a little more observant? I didn't have a thing to go by. Not even hair color. All I knew about my Secret Admirer was that he had nice shoes and either brown or red hair. Some clues.

There was no point in looking any further.

"What's going on?" asked the boy.

"Huh? Oh. . . . Well, see, this guy has been sending me notes signed 'Your Secret Admirer.'

And he's bought me presents and stuff, but I don't even know who he is."

"If you did, he wouldn't be a Secret Admirer," the boy pointed out. "He'd just be an admirer."

I smiled. "That's true."

"So who did you think you were chasing just now? I mean, what made you think that guy was your Secret Admirer?"

The boy and I were walking slowly through the hallway, heading for one of the open decks. I explained to him what had happened in the ice-cream parlor.

"You look pretty disappointed," said the boy.

I had just realized something else — my admirer was not Spider. If he was, Stacey would have recognized him for sure. She wouldn't have missed something like *that*. Darn. My admirer had vanished again and he wasn't Spider. A double blow. No wonder I looked disappointed.

But all I said to the boy was, "I just wanted to see him. That's all."

"Your admirer?"

"Yeah."

"Isn't it more fun if you don't know who he is?"

"Maybe. But in a few days this trip will be over and we'll be going home. I might not ever get to know him."

We'd reached the deck and were standing at the railing, looking out to sea. That day was the first one we'd had since the storm that wasn't perfectly clear. It wasn't overcast, but big, puffy clouds were looming on the horizon.

"Maybe he's shy."

"What?" My thoughts were drifting around like seaweed.

"Maybe your Secret Admirer is shy," said the boy. "Maybe he's afraid you won't like him, so he's being really nice to you before he introduces himself."

I brightened. "You know, I'll bet you're right! How come I didn't think of that? You're a complete stranger, and you have it all figured out."

"I'm a *boy*," said the boy.

I nodded. That made sense. "My name is Claudia," I told him.

"I'm Timothy."

We paused.

"So . . ." I said.

Why were we suddenly having trouble making conversation? It had seemed easier when we didn't know each other's names.

"So . . ." said Timothy.

I cleared my throat. "Where are you from?" Maybe he would be from someplace exotic like

116

Tahiti or Los Angeles. At least that would give us something to talk about.

"I'm from Connecticut," he replied. "How about you?"

"Hey, I'm from Connecticut, too! From Stoneybrook."

"No kidding. I'm from Darien. That's not too far from Stoneybrook."

My geography is terrible, so I wasn't sure, but I figured Timothy knew what he was talking about.

"Are you on this trip with your family?" I asked.

"Yup." Timothy nodded.

"Oh. I came with friends." I tried to explain about Kristy and her mom and Watson and the girls in the Baby-sitters Club, but I think I only confused him.

"Hey, I just thought of something," said Timothy. "When we're in high school, our football teams will play against each other. It's like we're destined to meet again."

Destined to meet again, I repeated to myself. What beautiful words. "Are you by any chance a, um, I mean, do you write poetry or something?" I had to ask the question, even if it was weird. See, the first guy I ever liked was named Trevor

Sandbourne, and he was a poet. It seemed that I was always falling for poets.

"Write poetry?" repeated Timothy.

"Yeah. I was just wondering. Because what you said — 'destined to meet again' — that was beautiful."

"Oh, thanks! Well, I like to write, but I'm no poet."

I nodded. I found myself studying Timothy's face. It was framed by curly hair. His eyes were dark, wide-set, and fringed with long lashes that I would have given my eye-teeth for. And he was the perfect height for me. . . . Wait a minute! What was I doing? I had a Secret Admirer. I didn't need Timothy, too. On the other hand, the admirer wasn't showing his face. And Timothy was awfully nice. Plus he wasn't in hiding.

"You know," I said, "I'm really glad I ran into you. I was looking for my Secret Admirer, and I found you instead. Maybe this was meant to happen."

"Kismet," agreed Timothy. I must have looked pretty blank because he added, "Fate."

"Destiny?"

"I guess."

I looked out over the ocean again. And this time I saw something I hadn't seen in several days. Land. Not just an island, but actual, honest-to-goodness *land*. Florida.

"Look!" I cried. "Port Canaveral. I feel like I'm home again, even though I've only been here once before and I'll probably never be back."

"I know what you mean," said Timothy.

"Tomorrow we'll be at Disney World," I went on, growing excited. "The beginning of three whole days of rides and junk food."

"Do you think, um, that maybe we could — we could spend some time together there?" asked Timothy, sounding awfully unsure of himself.

"Definitely," I answered. "That would be fun. Hey, listen, I better go. I don't know about you, but I'm not even packed. There's stuff all over our cabin. I've got to get ready to leave."

"I better go, too," said Timothy. He looked as if it were the last thing in the world he wanted to do.

"Walk me to my cabin, okay? Is it on your way? We're staying on the Dolphin Deck."

"It's not on my way, but I'll walk you anyway," said Timothy.

So he did. He left me at the door to my cabin, and I entered it to find the usual mess, only this time, the mess was all mine. Both Kristy and Dawn were already packed. They were lying on their bunks, each reading a book. The silence in the cabin was stony.

"I have just one thing to say," I said menacingly to my friends.

They looked up in surprise.

"What I have to say is that this is our last hour in this tiny cabin. When we get to our hotel, our room will be much bigger. There will be plenty of space for all of our stuff. So I expect the two of you to quit arguing and get along. Understand?"

The girls nodded, bewildered. I couldn't blame them. I didn't sound like myself at all. But I'd had just about as much of them as I could take.

CHAPTER 14

Kristy

Well, Claudia was right. Our hotel room sure was bigger than our cabin on the ship. It seemed like a palace in comparison. There were two closets, two giant dressers, and storage space under both sinks.

Both sinks. That was another thing. There were two bathrooms. Sort of. There was an actual bathroom with a shower and a toilet and a sink and everything, and then, just outside of it, there was a dressing room with another sink and a mirror and a cabinet. Very swank.

However, there was one problem — three of us, two beds. I took one look and said, "Who gets the bed to herself?" The beds were enormous. King-size, I guess.

At that point, Claudia put her foot down for the second time that day. "We are going to be here three nights," she said firmly. "So we'll switch off. Each of us will have a bed to herself one night. And I don't want any more contamination wars or clothes battles. There are plenty of drawers and coat hangers. We have enough space to put *all* of our stuff away, even mine. So let's do it. And then you two," she went on, glaring at Dawn and me, "are going to call a truce."

Dawn and I didn't dare to argue with Claudia. We started to unpack our things. Since we weren't talking, I switched on the TV. "Hey!" I said immediately. "We get cable here!"

"Really?" exclaimed Dawn, who doesn't have cable TV at her house in Connecticut. "Hey, maybe we'll get, you know, some movies we're not allowed to watch."

"R-rated?" I suggested, my eyes growing wide. "Yeah! Maybe." (We do have cable at home, but Watson won't let us get any of the movie channels. It's one of the few things he's strict about.) I started flipping channels, while Dawn opened a program guide she found on top of the TV.

"Darn," she said after a minute of flipping through it. "Nothing R-rated. Nothing worse than an old murder mystery. That's on Channel Eight, if you want to watch it."

I flipped to eight and we went back to our unpacking. When we were finished, we realized that Claudia was right again. There was plenty of room for all our stuff. Of course, Claudia had used up more drawers and hangers than Dawn and I together, but what did we care?

The room was as neat as a pin.

I couldn't resist. I opened a bag of Fritos that was in my knapsack, dumped them out on one of the bedside tables, and dropped the empty package on the floor.

Dawn made a face at me, then snatched up the bag and flung it in a wastebasket.

A hand closed over my Fritos. I looked up. Claudia was now making a face at me. "Kristin Amanda," she said. "You are . . . you are . . . What's the word? Goating her?"

"Goading her," I said sullenly.

"Right. You're goading Dawn and there's no reason for it. Come *on*. We've got this nice, tidy, *big* room. And we've got three days at Disney World ahead of us. It would be helpful if the two of you could get along. You'd have a much better time. So would you call a truce. *Please?*"

I looked at Dawn.

She looked at me.

"Truce?" I asked.

"Truce," she replied.

"Now shake on it," Claudia instructed.

Dawn and I glanced at Claudia, then at each other. Finally we shook hands. I know my hand was salty and greasy from the Fritos, but Dawn didn't say a word about it.

After we'd shaken, I started flipping TV dials again. The murder mystery was really boring.

"Kristy?" Dawn ventured. "Have you ever seen an R-rated movie?"

"Nah," I replied. "But someday I'm going to. Have you ever seen one?"

"Nah."

"Me neither," said Claudia, heading into the bathroom.

"My brother saw one once by accident," said Dawn. "He said it was no big deal."

"Really?"

"Yeah."

"What a disappointment."

Dawn and I began to laugh. "I bet we'll finally see one," said Dawn, "and after it's over we'll go, 'So what?' "

"Hey, you guys!" called Claudia from the bathroom. "Come here! There's more great free stuff."

Dawn jumped up, but I put my arm out to stop her. "I just want you to know," I said, "that I'm sorry about the way I acted. Sometimes I was being messier than usual. On purpose."

"I'm sorry, too," replied Dawn. "Sometimes *I* was being *neater* than usual. On purpose."

I gave Dawn a quick hug to show her that I really meant I was sorry, and then we joined Claudia in the bathroom.

"Look at this!" Claudia cried. "A shower cap, a shoe horn, a shoe buff, and this whole basket full of stuff — soap shaped like shells, shampoo, creme rinse, mouthwash, hand lotion, a sewing kit."

We explored the bedroom thoroughly then and found a local newspaper, some postcards and stationery, two ballpoint pens and —

"Whoa! Look at this!" cried Dawn. "How come we didn't notice this before? Look what the TV is standing on."

The TV was standing on a refrigerator. But we couldn't open it. It seemed to be locked. Next to it was a cabinet full of —

"JUNK FOOD!" shrieked Claudia. "Aughh! Candy bars and M&Ms and potato chips and pretzels. How do we get into this thing?"

We couldn't figure it out, so we called Watson in from the next room.

Watson took one look around, found a key which he said opened the refrigerator and the cabinet, and put it in his pocket. "Sorry, girls," he said. "I know the stuff in there looks tempting," (we hadn't even seen what was in the fridge), "but it costs an arm and a leg. I'm not kidding. It's probably two dollars for a fifty-cent bag of chips. That sort of thing. More than what you'd pay in any store. You'll do much better getting sodas from the machine down the hall and snacks from the shop in the lobby."

"Okay," we said, feeling let down. The idea of a stocked junk-food cabinet had been very appealing.

"Watson? Can we explore the hotel?" I asked. It was five o'clock in the afternoon. We wouldn't be going to Disney World until the next day.

"Sure," replied Watson. "I don't see why not. Just be back in time to get dressed for dinner. We're going to eat at seven, and we're going to a pretty fancy dining room here, so you'll have to change your clothes first."

(We were all wearing jeans.)

"No problem," I said. "Come on, you guys."

Watson cleared his throat. "How would you feel about taking Karen and Andrew with you?

They're dying to go exploring, too. Well, Karen is. Andrew just wants to do whatever she's doing."

I grinned. "No problem."

The five of us set off. We went to the lobby first. And what was the first thing we saw? Mr. Staples at the checkout desk.

"The check*out* desk!" I exclaimed. "Just a sec, you guys. I have to see what's going on."

I ran across the lobby. "Mr. Staples! Mr. Staples!" I called. "What are you doing?"

I reached him just as he was handing in his room key.

Mr. Staples looked at me in surprise. "What am I doing?" he repeated. "I'm checking out, that's what. Going home."

"Buy *why*?" I pressed.

"Whole trip was a darn-fool idea," he said. "Shouldn't have come."

"But we had fun playing Donkey Kong and shuffleboard, didn't we? And I have to tell you something very important about that fight I was having with Dawn." Mr. Staples and I had discussed it several more times on the cruise, and he'd been really helpful, considering he was a slob like me. We'd talked about his wife a lot, too, and I'd thought he'd seemed a little more cheerful. "And," I went on, "my parents really liked eating dinner with you. Besides, I haven't given you Nannie's phone number yet."

"Plus," said Karen, who had joined us, "remember at dinner? You said you'd pull a quarter out of my ear? Well, you didn't do it yet."

"I thought we were going to spend some time together at Disney World," I added, truly disappointed. "And you wanted to get Mickey Mouse ears for your grandchildren and have their names put on them."

"Okay, okay, okay!" Mr. Staples threw up his hands, but he was smiling. "I know when I'm licked."

I didn't leave his side until he had the room key in his pocket again. Then Dawn and Claudia and Karen and Andrew and I did go exploring. We returned to our rooms and finished getting dressed just five minutes before dinner. Andrew put on a suit. Karen put on a party dress. They looked so snazzy that I took their picture.

After dinner we managed to hold a quick Baby-sitters Club meeting, but everyone was tired, and no one had any ideas about presents for Mom and Watson and the Pikes, not any decent ideas, that is.

"We're running out of time," I told my friends.

"We know, we know," they replied. But the added pressure only made us more nervous, not more creative.

When I went to bed that night, I was exhausted.

CHAPTER 15

Karen

Disney World! Disney World! Disney World! This is my dream! I have always, always wanted to come here. Ever since I first saw a TV commercial about it.

I went with Daddy, Elizabeth, and Andrew the next day. I wanted Kristy to come with us, but she decided to walk around with Claudia. And David Michael went off with his big brothers.

It took a long time to get from our hotel to Disney World. First we took a bus to a gigantic parking lot. Then we rode on a monorail to Disney World. The monorail was fun. It was way up high. I felt like we were on a flying train.

When we got off the monorail — Disney World! We gave a lady our tickets and pushed through a turnstile and suddenly we were on Main Street.

"Oooh," I said. "Look. We're in a little town. Right here in Disney World."

An old-fashioned fire truck came down the street. So did a horse-drawn buggy. We were standing at the town square. I could see a popcorn machine and —

"Look!" shrieked Andrew. "It's Minnie Mouse! I see Minnie Mouse! She's right over there. And she's signing autographs!"

"Oh, Daddy, Daddy, Daddy, please can we go see Minnie?" I begged. "I swear, she is my best friend in the whole wide world."

Daddy raised his eyebrows. "She is?"

She really wasn't, and we both knew it. But I just had to get Minnie's autograph. And maybe have my picture taken with her.

I grabbed Daddy by the hand, and Andrew grabbed Elizabeth by the hand. We pulled them across the square to Minnie. Some other kids were standing with her, and Minnie was leaning over and patting their heads. The kids were giggling. Their parents snapped pictures. Then Minnie waved good-bye to them.

And what did she do next? She waved to my brother and me!

Andrew and I looked at each other.

"Go on over," whispered Daddy, giving me a little push forward.

I took Andrew's hand and led him to Minnie Mouse. I felt excited and scared. It was just like visiting Santa Claus at the department store. When we reached Minnie's side, she shook our hands.

"Hi, Minnie! Hi, Minnie!" I said.

"Hi, Minnie," whispered Andrew.

Minnie waved again. I guess she doesn't talk.

I opened up my pink purse and took out a pad of paper and a pen. I handed them to Minnie. "Please could you give us your autograph?" I asked. "And could you write one for each of us?"

Minnie wrote this on two pieces of paper: *LOVE MINNIE MOUSE* Then she gave the pad back to me. I looked at the papers in awe. Andrew and I had Minnie Mouse's autograph! We would be famous in Stoneybrook. I sure hoped we would have Show-and-Tell when school started again, because boy, would I have something to show!

I gave Andrew his autograph and Minnie put her arms around us.

"Smile!" called Daddy.

Andrew and I smiled while Minnie hugged us tightly. Then she patted us on our heads and sent us back to Daddy and Elizabeth.

"Good-bye!" we called.

"Say thank-you," whispered Daddy.

"Thanks!" we cried.

We walked along Main Street.

"Look! Look at everything!" I exclaimed. I began reading the names on the stores. "House of Magic. Penny Arcade, The Shadow Box, Main Street Cinema, The Con . . . Con . . ."

"Confectionary," Elizabeth told me.

"What's that?" I asked.

Elizabeth and Daddy glanced at each other. "It's a candy store," said my stepmother.

"Andrew! Andrew! A candy store!" I screeched. "Daddy, can we go in?"

"Wait!" said Andrew. "There's a man selling Mickey Mouse balloons. Can we have one?"

"Can we get ice-cream cones?" I asked.

"Can we go to the movie theater?" asked Andrew.

"Can we buy magic tricks?" I asked as we passed by the House of Magic.

"Whoa! Whoa!" exclaimed Daddy. "Hold on, kids. We'll try to do everything. I promise. But we can only do one thing at a time. Since we're here, let's go to the magic store."

"Goody!" I said. "Come on, Andrew."

The magic store was dark, but it was filled with great stuff. There were jokes like rubber spiders, and magic tricks like handkerchiefs that turned into eggs. And there were masks and disguises, too.

"You may choose one thing each," said Daddy.

I chose the handkerchief egg. Andrew chose the spider. It was attached to a rubber ball. When you squeezed the ball, the spider jumped. Andrew took it out of the package and made it jump for Elizabeth. She screamed. We all laughed.

Then we started walking down Main Street again. Daddy bought us balloons and ice-cream cones. I could hardly eat my cone, though. I was too excited. That was because when we reached the end of Main Street, the Cinderella Castle stood before us. It was huge, and it looked just like a castle in a fairy tale.

"Oooh," I breathed. "It's beautiful."

"Does Cinderella really live there?" Andrew wondered.

I was about to say, "Of course not, silly," when I realized I wasn't sure myself. Andrew and I looked at Daddy.

"Well . . ." Daddy said slowly. "I'm afraid not. But it's still a pretty nice castle, isn't it?"

"Look at the turrets," said Elizabeth.

"The flags," said Daddy.

"The crenellation," added Elizabeth.

I was too excited to bother to ask about crenellation. Besides, it was time to make a decision. From where we were standing, we could walk right to Tomorrowland, Liberty Square, or Adventureland.

"Daddy?" I said. "Where's the Haunted Mansion? Can we go to the Haunted Mansion?" Kristy had been telling me about all the rides at Disney World, and the one I wanted to go on the most was the Haunted Mansion. Space Mountain sounded like a good roller coaster, Peter Pan's Flight sounded fun, Snow White's Scary Adventures sounded maybe just a *little* scary, but the Haunted Mansion sounded like the ride for me.

I happen to know a lot about spooky stuff. At Daddy's house in Stoneybrook, there's a ghost on the third floor — old Ben Brewer. And next door lives a witch named Morbidda Destiny.

Daddy took a map out of his pocket. "You're in luck, Karen," he said. "The Haunted Mansion is nearby. It's in Liberty Square. Over this way."

We began walking. Just when I thought I could see the house on a hill not far away, I heard a horrible, moaning scream. "Oooo-weee-ooooo . . ."

"What was that?" I shrieked.

I heard the scream again.

Elizabeth laughed. "I think it's coming from the Haunted Mansion, honey. We're in for a scary ride."

"I hope so," I said, but I said it in a very small voice. And I reached out and held tightly to Elizabeth's hand.

Andrew was so scared that Daddy had to carry him.

We walked up a path to a spooky old mansion. We began to pass tombstones. A line of people had formed at the front door to the house, so while we waited in line, I looked at the little graveyard.

"Dear departed Brother Dave," I read to Elizabeth from one of the tombs.

"He chased a bear into a cave," she finished.

I giggled. Then I read another. "Here lies good old Fred. A great big rock fell on his head. R.I.P." I knew what R.I.P. meant — rest in peace.

The line began to move and we walked slowly

into a dim room. The whole crowd of people took a ride down in a weird elevator. When we got off we climbed into little black cars. The cars were heading into darkness. I got into a car with Elizabeth. Andrew and Daddy climbed into the car behind us.

The ride began. It wasn't a wild ride that jerked you around corners or turned you upside down. Instead, the cars took us on a tour through the most haunted house I could imagine. We saw ghosts dancing in a cobwebby ballroom. We saw a face appear in a crystal ball. We saw wallpaper with bats' eyes all over it, and a scary, scary graveyard — much scarier than the one outside.

All the time we were riding, a deep voice was telling us about the spooks in the mansion. Just when I thought the ride was over, the voice said something about hitchhiking ghosts.

"Hitchhiking ghosts?" I whispered to Elizabeth. She shrugged.

And at that moment we passed a wall of mirrors. I looked for our car. "There we are!" I said. "Look, Elizabeth. There — Hey! Aughh!"

I couldn't help screaming. When I looked in the mirror, I could see that Elizabeth and I were not alone. Sitting between us, right in our car, was . . . a ghost!

"We've got a ghost! A ghost is next to us!" I shrieked.

We reached the end of the mirrors. The ride was over. But the ghost was still in our car. I was terrified.

"It was just a trick, sweetie," Elizabeth said. "That ghost was a hologram. It wasn't really there."

"I don't care what it's called," I said as we left the Haunted Mansion. "It was real. I saw it. And I know it's still with us. I can feel my ghost. He's making my skin creep." I shivered.

"Let's go to Fantasyland," said Daddy. "That won't be so scary."

So we headed for Fantasyland. The first thing that happened there was that Andrew's shoelace came untied. He stooped down to fix it. When he straightened up, Snow White was standing next to him. She was just walking around Disney World like Minnie Mouse had been. But I guess Andrew wasn't expecting to see her.

"Wahh!" he cried, bursting into tears.

Snow White felt terrible. You could tell.

It was a long time before Andrew calmed down.

Then we went on lots of rides in Fantasyland. But you know what?

My ghost wouldn't leave me alone. He came along with me on every one. Nobody could see him except me. I could feel my skin creeping all afternoon.

CHAPTER 16

Dawn

Guess what? Last night I ran into Parker in the hotel after dinner, and he asked if I wanted to spend our first day at the Magic Kingdom together. Why did he even bother asking? Of course I did!

I got permission from Kristy's mom, and Parker and I met in the lobby at 10:00 the next morning.

I felt so grown-up I absolutely cannot describe it.

Claudia had helped me get dressed. She was in a great mood because her Secret Admirer had left her a stuffed animal at the door to our room during the night. Since she had brought along nearly every article of clothing that she owns, and I'd only brought along about one thirty-second of my wardrobe, I borrowed a few of her things. In fact, I borrowed the entire outfit. (We're just about the same size.) Parker would never know. I mean, he'd never know the outfit was borrowed, not that Claudia and I are the same size.

This is the outfit Claudia helped me to choose: a white tank top under lavender overalls, lavender push-down socks, lavender high-top sneakers, and a beaded belt, which we looped droopily twice around my middle. In my hair we put lavender-and-white clips that looked like birds. I thought they were just any kind of bird, but Claudia swore up and down that they were birds of paradise. Who knows? (I think she was making that up.)

Anyway, if I do say so myself (and I do), I looked pretty nice when I met Parker.

Parker wasn't looking bad, either. He was wearing this blue-and-white polo shirt, white tennis shorts, and loafers with no socks.

"I hope your shoes are comfortable," I said to him. "We're going to be walking around all day. They won't wear blisters on your heels or anything, will they?"

"Nope," he replied. "Not these old things. They're ready to fall apart any second."

"Well, as long as they can hold together one more day."

"No problem. You got your ticket?"

I held it up. "Yup," I replied. Everybody on the trip had a three-day pass to Disney World and Epcot Center.

"Great," said Parker. "Let's go."

There was free bus service from our hotel to the Magic Kingdom, so we waited in front of the hotel for a bus. The bus took us to the parking lot at Disney World, which was the biggest lot I have ever seen — except for the one at Disneyland in California. I'd already been to Disneyland ten or twelve times because I used to live not far from it. I had a feeling Disney World wasn't going to be all that different — but going to it with a boy would be.

The parking lot is so far away from the entrance to the Magic Kingdom that after you get off the bus, you have to get on a monorail that takes you to the gates. It seemed like forever before we were walking down Main Street in the Magic Kingdom, but we had left the hotel less than an hour earlier.

"Wow," said Parker, looking around in awe. "This is a whole town right in the park. And it's really only a little piece of Disney World."

"Yeah," I agreed. Main Street in Disney

World looked pretty much like Main Street in Disneyland.

"You don't seem too excited," said Parker vaguely.

I tried to be more enthusiastic. "Well!" I said. "What should we do first? There's a magic store! And there's a movie house!"

"Uh, let's get to the rides," said Parker quickly. "Main Street looks like fun, but we can go to stores or the movies any time. Come on. Let's find Space Mountain. It's supposed to be really cool."

"Okay," I said, but since I'd been on Space Mountain at Disneyland nine times, I couldn't work up to Parker's level of excitement.

We walked away from Main Street, turned right by Cinderella Castle, and entered Tomorrowland. It was a sea of smooth, white, futuristic-looking buildings. And ahead of us loomed Space Mountain. Since it was still pretty early in the day, the line for the ride wasn't too long. But we did have to wait about twenty minutes.

At last, though, Parker and I were climbing into the cars. Were they called spacejets or something? I wasn't sure. Parker sat in front and I sat in back. An attendant strapped us in.

The car moved forward toward darkness. We could hear people above us — those who were already on the ride — screaming and shrieking.

"Hold on to your hat!" yelled Parker, and we were immediately jerked around a corner.

For the next three minutes, we got the ride of our lives. I swear, Space Mountain at Disney World is nothing like Space Mountain at Disneyland. I felt *much* more like I was on a roller coaster hurtling through outer space. A lot of the ride took place in pitch blackness. I couldn't even see if the track ahead went up or down. A few times, we were traveling so fast I thought my face was going to be permanently mashed in. Then we went down one hill that was so steep I was positive my stomach had fallen right out of my body.

I almost threw up.

We whizzed through a bright red tunnel. Parker couldn't turn around to look at me, but he waved over his shoulder.

Parker was waving, and I was having a hard time just keeping my breakfast down. We zoomed around some more, and several times I was *sure* our car was going to fly off the track and crash somewhere. But of course it didn't.

Still, by the time the ride was over, my knees were shaking, and Parker had to help me out of the spacejet.

"You okay?" he asked, looking worried.

I tried to come up with an answer that wasn't too disgusting. As we left the ride, traveling along a moving walkway, I decided not to say, "No, I'm about to puke all over you," or, "I'm fine, but how'd you like to see what I had for breakfast this morning?"

Instead, I replied, "Well, um, can we not do that again?"

Parker laughed. But he was concerned. When we left Space Mountain, we found a spot to sit down and Parker bought us each a soda. He made me wait until mine was sort of flat before I began sipping it. By the time I was finished, I felt lots better — but not good enough to try another ride.

We settled on strolling from store to store, even though Parker had been right: we could shop anywhere.

"But not for the perfect Disney World souvenir," I pointed out.

"That's true. Is that what we're doing?"

"Don't you think we should? Who knows when we'll be back here again."

So we started looking. The only problem was that I had just $8.60 left, and I didn't want some little pennant or sticker. I wanted something nice. I finally found the perfect thing in the gift shop in Cinderella Castle. It was a glass unicorn charm, and it cost only six dollars. After I'd paid for it, Parker helped me fasten it to this gold bracelet I was wearing. The bracelet used to belong to my great-aunt. It's an antique, and when Mom gave it to me, she said that whatever I did, I was to keep it in the family. I'm not sure how much money it's worth, but it has a lot of sentimental value. The charm looked great on it.

Anyway, then Parker bought a T-shirt for himself. (I guess boys don't care so much about souvenirs.)

By that time, I was feeling fine again. In fact, I was hungry. As we walked through Frontierland looking for a place to eat, Parker suddenly stopped in his tracks and said, "Uh-oh."

"What-oh?"

"It's my family," Parker told me. "My dad, the stepmother, and the brats."

I looked where Parker was pointing and saw a very nice-looking man and woman and two cute little boys.

"Parker!" called the man.

Parker groaned and led me over to his father. There were introductions all around. And then Mr. Harris said the last thing I'd expected to hear:

"Patsy and I are exhausted. We'd love a little break. Would you mind watching the boys for an hour or so, Parker?"

What could Parker say? We agreed to take the boys and meet Mr. and Mrs. Harris in an hour and a half at Cinderella Castle.

The Harrises left. Parker and I looked at the boys — Roddy, who was eight and Ricky, who was five. They didn't seem like brats to me.

Since Parker was acting like children were aliens from another planet, I said to the boys, "So what do you guys want to do?"

"Could we go on Big Thunder Mountain Railroad?" asked Roddy. "Please?"

"Sure," replied Parker.

"But it looks scary," said Ricky nervously.

Parker relaxed a little. "It won't be too bad," he said.

"Will you sit with me?" asked Ricky. He held his hand out to Parker.

I gave Parker a look that said, "*These* are the *brats* you've been complaining about?"

Parker shrugged.

We got on line for the railroad, which I knew

was another roller coaster, but not nearly as wild as Space Mountain. Since I hadn't eaten lunch yet, my stomach could handle it.

Ricky and Roddy screamed from the beginning of the ride until the end. They clutched our hands. They loved every second of it.

"Can we go again?" asked Roddy before we'd even gotten out of the mining car we'd been riding in.

"We could," Parker told him, "but don't you want to do something new? Have you been to Tom Sawyer Island yet?" (Parker looked like he was actually having fun with his stepbrothers.)

"No," said Ricky.

"Well, let's go!" said Parker.

So we went. We took a raft over to the island, which turned out to be more like a park, and Ricky and Roddy had a blast. There were hills to climb and a cave to explore and a wobbly bridge made of barrels to walk across. But they had the most fun firing off these air guns at Fort Sam Clemens.

By the time we had to leave to meet Parker's father and stepmother, the four of us were laughing and talking happily — until I realized that my unicorn charm and bracelet were missing.

I burst into tears. Who knew where I'd lost them? And I could never replace the bracelet. Mom was going to kill me. Plus, I only had $2.50 left. Not enough for a new charm. So the day was sort of ruined. But I did feel an awful lot better when, returning to the hotel later, Parker reached into his pocket and handed me something wrapped in tissue paper.

I opened it. It was another unicorn.

I was so pleased and so surprised that I started to cry again.

Parker blushed.

And then he kissed me on the cheek.

CHAPTER 17

Mallory

I don't know about this spying business. See, the frustrating thing is that sometimes you see or overhear things you don't understand, can't figure out, or never learn anything more about. For instance, what about that stowaway I saw the first day we were aboard the *Ocean Princess*? I spent the entire trip waiting for someone to discover him and arrest him. But nothing like that happened at all. The most exciting part of the trip was the storm we had one night. A big wave rocked the ship, and Vanessa's shoes flew through the air and hit Mary Anne on the head.

What had happened to the pretty girl who looked like she might be from New York? I'd never seen her again. I knew that her name was Alexandra Carmody, that she'd talked to Mary

Anne a few times, that she'd said she was an orphan, an actress, a countess's niece or something, and that she was traveling alone, which was all pretty interesting. But I hadn't seen her.

And where was Spider from the Insects, for heaven's sake? You'd think I would have seen *him* again.

I did know something more about the little boy in the wheelchair and the old man. The boy, Marc Kubacki, had become a friend of Stacey, Claire, and Margo, and the man, Mr. Staples, had become a friend of Kristy Thomas. But I wanted to know about the others.

I got my chance for more spying the very first day we went to the Magic Kingdom. After spending the morning together as one big group — Mom, Dad, all my brothers and sisters, me, Mary Anne, and Stacey — my parents said we could split up when lunch was over. I begged to be allowed to go off on my own again.

"Your own?" said Dad, frowning. "You really want to go on rides by yourself? Wouldn't you have more fun with some of your brothers and sisters — or even your old dad?"

I grinned. "Don't worry about me . . . Old Dad. I'll go on rides again with everyone tomorrow. This afternoon I just want to look around. I might go shopping or to one of the shows. And the parade comes down Main Street in the afternoon. I don't want to miss that."

"A parade?" exclaimed Claire. "There's going to be a *parade*? Oh, please, please, please can we go?"

"Sure," replied my mother, "but you might like it better at night. They hold the parade at night, too. And later, fireworks go off."

"Fireworks! Like on the Fourth of July? Oh, let's go at night!" This time it was Margo who was so excited.

"Well, anyway," I interrupted, "so it's all right if I spend the afternoon on my own? I'm kind of looking forward to it."

My parents exchanged a glance. At last Mom said, "I think it's all right. But we're going to meet at five o'clock at Cinderella Castle. And if you're not there, I'm going to be *very worried*."

"I'll be there," I promised.

Mom smiled. "Let's figure out how the rest of us are going to split up," she said. Then she made the mistake that's always made at least once whenever us Pikes are on vacation. She said, "What does everyone want to do?"

"Go on Pirates of the Caribbean," said Byron.

"Go on Mr. Toad's Wild Ride again," said Margo.

"Go on Space Mountain again," said Jordan.

"Go on the spinning teacups," said Nicky.

"Go on It's a Small World," said Vanessa.

"Ride the skyway," said Adam.

"Get an ice-cream cone," said Claire. "And a Mickey Mouse balloon."

Mom looked at Dad. "Ride the merry-go-round," he said, and everybody laughed.

I left them behind, trying to sort out who was going to go with whom, taking into consideration things like: Mary Anne refused to ride the skyway because it was so high up, the spinning teacup ride would make Margo barf, etc.

As soon as I was safely out of sight of my family, I sat down on a bench and pulled out my spying notebook. As far as I knew, no one had looked in it or even found it. I uncapped a pen and started making some notes:

Two old ladies walk by. They have blue hair.

A family walks by with a kid in a stroller. The kid is crying.

Another family goes by. The little girl drops her ice-cream cone. Cries.

A big group of people goes by. They are wearing matching T-shirts. They are very loud (the people, not the shirts). Having fun. Lots of smiles.

A family goes by. Both kids crying.

(How come all the kids are crying? I check my watch. It is naptime.)

Two parents and a little girl come by. The girl's legs are in braces. She doesn't seem to care. She is saying, "Snow White's Scary Adventure is the funnest ride here!"

This was all very interesting, and it might help improve my writing skills and sharpen my powers of observation, but it wasn't true spying. At any rate, it wasn't the kind of spying Harriet would have done. Harriet would have dug up secrets. I was just watching crying children.

I decided to find a better place to spy. Maybe I could sit down somewhere in Fantasyland next to a line for a ride. That way, I could overhear conversations. Now *that* would be interesting.

I headed for Fantasyland. When I got there, I realized I had just one problem. There was no place to sit down that was near enough to a line so that I could actually listen in on conversations.

I sighed.

Then I kind of hung around lines for awhile. I heard a kid tell his father he was tired of waiting. (Big deal.) I heard a little girl say she was starved and ask for ice cream. (Is that the *only* thing children want to eat at Disney World?) And I heard one old man tell an old woman that he'd been through the Haunted Mansion six times. (Yawn.)

And *then* I saw Alexandra Carmody, the beautiful girl from the *Ocean Princess*! She was just as beautiful as ever, with that long, wavy hair. And she seemed to have found some friends — a light-haired boy who looked a little younger than she, and an older couple. Maybe the boy's parents?

Now I had something to find out about!

They joined the end of the line for Peter Pan's Flight, so I got on the line right behind them, even though I'd just been on Peter Pan's Flight that morning.

I poised my pen and opened my ears.

But for the longest time, none of them spoke. Maybe they were really, really tired. I capped my pen again.

Spying can be a bore.

Finally the boy said, "Hey, Mom, remember when you read *Peter Pan* to us?"

So the man and woman *were* the boy's parents — or at least, the woman was his mother.

"I certainly do," the woman replied fondly. "Captain Hook scared you two so much you had nightmares. Remember, Alex?"

Alex? I didn't get it. The woman was talking like she was Alexandra's mother. But Alexandra wasn't supposed to have any parents.

"Oh, don't remind me, Mom!" Alex cried. "Hey, Daddy —" (She tugged at the sleeve of the man's shirt.) "— I made you hide my alarm clock. Remember? I said it scared me as much as it scared Captain Hook."

"Some big sister you were," the boy added, but you could tell he was kidding. "You were more scared of everything than I was."

Mom, Daddy, big sister!

Boy, what a liar Alexandra was! She told Mary Anne she was an orphan — that her parents had been killed — and here she was with her parents and her brother.

Just when I thought I'd had all the surprises I could handle, I noticed that a couple in front of Alexandra's parents, who were about the same age as the Carmodys, were whispering and nudging each other. Every so often, they'd turn around to look at Mr. and Mrs. Carmody.

I couldn't tell whether the Carmodys saw them or not — but they couldn't help but notice when the woman finally said, "Excuse me, but are you Viv and Vernon Carmody?"

Now why did those names sound familiar?

The Carmodys smiled graciously. "Yes, we are," said Alex's father.

"Oh, I have to tell you!" the woman exclaimed. "My husband and I are your biggest fans. We have been for years. Are you performing here at Disney World?"

I listened and gawked and scribbled notes. I figured out who the Carmodys were — a man and wife singing team who were popular with people my parents' age and older. I knew I'd heard their names before. I think Mom and Dad even have one of their albums.

But, boy, was I left with a lot of questions. The biggest one was, why was Alexandra such a liar? I couldn't wait to find Mary Anne and tell her what I had learned!

CHAPTER 18

Mary Anne

What a day our first day at the Magic Kingdom was. I was exhausted. I thought the Pike kids wore Stacey and me out when we went to Sea City, but that was nothing compared to a day at Disney World. My feet ached, my back ached, and my head ached. I'd been on Space Mountain twice, Big Thunder Mountain Railroad three times, and I'd stood on miles of lines. Then Kristy had called a club meeting for right after dinner. And ever since we'd met the Pikes at Cinderella Castle that afternoon, Mallory had been bugging me about something. She kept saying she wanted to talk to me, but that we had to talk in private.

"Okay," I said. We were back at the hotel and I was rummaging around in my suitcase, looking for aspirin. "We'll talk when I get back from the club meeting. Your mom gave Stacey and me an hour and a half off, so I'll talk to you right before we go to bed."

"What about Vanessa?" asked Mallory.

"We'll wait until she's in the bathroom. You know she takes forever. Is that okay?" I asked.

Mallory nodded.

"Great," I said. But I was wishing that I could just fall into bed, go to sleep right then, and not get up until the next morning. Or maybe the next afternoon.

Instead, I dragged myself to the club meeting. Stacey dragged along with me. She was as tired as I was.

The meeting was held in the room Kristy, Claudia, and Dawn were sharing. When we entered, I drew in my breath in surprise. Their cabin on the ship had looked like the back end of a garbage truck. But their hotel room looked like, well, a hotel room. It was reasonably neat. There were no clothes lying around. There were no M&M wrappers on the floor or cracker crumbs on the desk. And Dawn and Kristy were actually smiling — at each other.

"Hi, you guys!" called Kristy as we entered the room.

"Hi," we replied.

"What's the matter?" Claudia asked us.

"We're exhausted," said Stacey.

"We're *baby*-sitting," I reminded them crossly.

"Touchy, touchy," said Dawn, who's the only one I would have let get away with saying something like that just then.

"Sit down," said Kristy. "Rest your feet. You want a soda or something?"

"Definitely," I answered.

Claudia looked longingly at a refrigerator and a cabinet that was full of potato chips and candy. "If only we could get in *there*," she said, touching her finger to the keyhole of the cabinet.

"Well, you know what Watson said," Kristy told her.

"Yeah," replied Claudia. "It's just . . ." She peered into the cabinet. "Oh, my lord, there's a Mounds bar way in the back! I haven't seen Mounds bars anywhere in the hotel. They're not in the store in the lobby."

"Claudia, that thing probably costs about twelve dollars. Come on. I've got Fritos and pretzels here. And I got some sodas out of the machine. Now let's start the meeting." Kristy was growing impatient.

She passed around sodas and opened the bags of pretzels and Fritos. We talked about the kids for awhile, but there wasn't much to say. They were all having a ball. Kristy mentioned that Karen thought she had a ghostly companion, but none of us knew what to do about that.

Dawn told us how she'd lost her bracelet, and grew teary-eyed.

Claudia showed Stacey and me a pair of barrettes her Secret Admirer had sent her at dinner.

Then I said that Claire and Margo were upset because we'd missed both the afternoon and the evening parades that day.

"You too?" said Kristy. "So did we. And Karen and Andrew missed them, too. They really wanted to see them. Or at least one of them. Did *any*one see one?"

We all shook our heads.

"Well, we'll remember tomorrow," said Kristy. "Now. Who has an idea for gifts for Mom and Watson and the Pikes?"

There were a few red faces among us. I knew we hadn't been thinking about the gifts at all.

Dawn cleared her throat. "I saw some really nice cement planters in the gift shop. They were shaped like turtles and —"

"Those huge things?!" cried Kristy. "They weigh a ton! How would we ever get them on the plane?"

Dawn shrugged, embarrassed.

"I saw some keychains in the shop," I said. "They were personalized. You could get them with almost any name. I found most of our names down there. I bet we could find —"

"Those keychains had Mickey Mouse on them, for heaven's sake!" said Kristy. "Get real, you baby-sitters. We want to do something special."

"Well, what ideas have you come up with?" I asked.

"No good ones," said Kristy. "But they were better than cement planters and Mickey Mouse keychains."

"There's a nice clothing store in the lobby," Claudia began.

"You guys are missing the point," interrupted Kristy. "We don't want to give just any gift. We don't even want to give just an expensive gift. We have to give meaningful gifts."

"Like what?" asked Stacey.

Kristy shrugged. "I don't know. Yet. Well, keep thinking."

We turned our attention to the Fritos. Then we found a Michael J. Fox movie on TV and tuned in.

I fell asleep.

I didn't wake up until I became aware that Stacey was shaking me gently and saying, "Mary Anne, Mary Anne, get up. Our break is over."

Stacey and I dragged ourselves back to our rooms.

As soon as I opened the door to mine, Mallory bounced over to me. (Where did she get all that energy?)

"Perfect timing!" she said. "Vanessa just went into the bathroom. I figure we have, oh, fifteen, twenty minutes."

"Okay." I lowered myself onto my bed. (Mallory and Vanessa were sharing the other bed.)

Mallory plunked herself down next to me. "I have some very important information," she began.

"Important information?" I said. "You sound like a spy, Mal."

For just a moment, I thought Mallory was blushing. But it was hard to tell. She'd gotten a lot of sun that day.

Mallory cleared her throat. "Well, anyway, guess who I just happened to be standing behind on the line for Peter Pan's Flight today?"

"I can't guess. Who?"

"Alexandra Carmody. And she was on line with her *mother*, her *father*, and her *brother*. I couldn't help overhearing what they were saying. And get this — her parents are, like, celebrities. Have you ever heard of Viv and Vernon Carmody? They're a singing team. They're for older people."

The names sounded vaguely familiar, but I couldn't think about names just then. All I could think was that Alex had parents.

"Are you sure about all this?" I asked Mallory.

"Positive. We were on line for half an hour. And I was right behind them."

"What a liar!" I cried. "Oh — I don't mean you, Mal. I mean Alex. She told me she was an *orphan*. And a whole bunch of other things. I wonder if *any* of it is true. Oh, who cares? But why did she tell me her parents are dead instead of celebrities? People shouldn't joke about things like that."

Mallory shook her head. "I thought you should know."

"Thanks," I replied. "I'm not sure what I'm going to do, but I am glad to know."

Even though I was tired, I didn't sleep well that night. I kept waking up and thinking about Alex. By morning, I had made one decision. The next time I saw her, I would confront Alex with what I knew.

Which happened to be during breakfast. Vanessa forgot to bring her vitamin pills to the dining room so I said I'd get them. I'd gotten as far as the lobby when I ran into Alex. I didn't bother to smile or say good morning to her. Instead, I greeted her with, "You . . . are . . . a . . . *liar.*" I proceeded to tell her everything Mallory had told me.

"But . . . but . . ." Alex kept saying. Her face crumpled up as if she were going to cry.

Usually I can't stand to see someone cry. I get all mushy and sympathetic. But that time, I turned my back and walked away. Alex had lied, and I'd opened up and told her about my mother, and now I felt like a fool. Worse, I felt hurt.

I hadn't seen the last of Alex, though. The Pikes and Stacey and I went back to the Magic Kingdom that morning and split into groups again. I wound up with Margo and Claire.

"Snow White! Snow White!" cried Claire. "Let's go on that ride again. I want to see the wicked witch."

So we went to Fantasyland and found Snow White's Scary Adventure. And who should get on line behind us but Alex.

"Hi, there," she said.

I didn't answer her. My hurt had turned to anger.

"Can't I even talk to you?" asked Alex. "I have to tell you something."

"What was your favorite part of this ride?" I asked Margo, ignoring Alex.

"Oh, easy. When the witch looks like she's going to push the big rock on you."

Alex stopped talking.

She came on the ride with us, though. I mean, climbed right into our little Dopey car, as if she were the fourth person in our party!

After the ride I tried to lose her in the crowd. When I thought I'd succeeded I said to the girls, "Have you guys been on Cinderella's Golden Carousel?"

"Nope," they replied.

So we stood on line, and then ran onto the merry-go-round and chose our horses. The music started. The horses began to move. As my horse rose up, the one next to me sank down. I found myself looking into Alex's face.

"Hi!" she said.

I whipped my head around and wouldn't pay attention to her.

A few minutes later, when the merry-go-round had slowed to a stop, Claire began begging for ice cream. I knew from experience that she wouldn't stop until she'd had some. We walked to The Round Table and each got a cone piled high with swirls of soft vanilla ice cream.

Alex stood on line behind us.

Purely to escape her, I walked the girls all the way over to Tomorrowland after we'd finished our cones. The first thing I noticed was a sign at Space Mountain announcing that the line was only ten minutes long. The second thing I noticed was that we'd finally lost Alexandra.

"This is the time to ride Space Mountain," I told the girls. "Hardly any wait."

"Goody!" they cried.

So we rode the roller coaster.

When we came out, Alex was waiting for us.

"There you are!" she said.

And at that moment, Margo threw up her

entire ice-cream cone and probably all of her breakfast, too. Most of it went on Alex's shoes.

That was the last we saw of Alexandra Carmody that day.

I couldn't have been happier.

CHAPTER 19

Byron

Disney World is awesome! And today is even better than yesterday was. That's because me and my brothers asked if David Michael could spend the day with us, and if we could be on our own again — us five boys — like we were at Treasure Cay.

Mom and Dad said no to being on our own, but yes to David Michael. That was good enough for me. I didn't care if Stacey had to follow us around. She's pretty cool. And she said we could do whatever we wanted as long as it was legal.

Well, we knew exactly what we wanted to do. The question was, would there be enough time for everything? We wanted to go on Space Mountain, Pirates of the Caribbean, the Haunted Mansion, and the rides in Frontierland. We wanted to look for hidden treasure again, too. (We still had our map.) And we wanted to eat as much food as possible.

"In that case," said Stacey, "there's just one thing I insist on."

"What?" I asked.

"That you ride Space Mountain and Big Thunder Mountain Railroad before you eat a *thing*. Got it?"

"Got it," we said.

That was a great excuse to go right to Space Mountain. It was early in the day and the line wasn't too long, so as soon as we came out of the ride, we went back in again.

"Oh," groaned Stacey. "Twice in a row? I don't think my poor old stomach is up to this."

"Well, you don't have to come with us. You could wait outside," I said hopefully.

"No way," replied Stacey. But she looked pretty green by the time we'd ridden Space Mountain the second time.

"Now — on to Big Thunder Mountain Railroad!" cried David Michael Thomas. "That's my favorite ride. You have to look around while you're on it. It's like you're really in the wild, wild west. Did you guys see the bones? And the possums hanging from the tree? And the chick-

170

ens and the goat? How about the mine shaft? I liked going up, up, up and then —"

"Oh, please!" said Stacey. "I know I told you we had to go on the roller coasters first, but I take it back. Let's find a tamer ride. We'll go on the railroad at the end of the day — if you haven't eaten too much."

"Pirates of the Caribbean!" I cried. "Let's go, you guys. Off to Adventureland!"

"Pirates of the Caribbean," Stacey repeated weakly. "Isn't that a water ride? I don't know. A boat . . . All that swaying and rocking . . ."

But we were already way ahead of her.

Stacey caught up to us as we were following the line through the caverns that lead to the beginning of the ride.

"This ride isn't bad," I whispered to Stacey, pulling her aside. "It's not like being on the water at all. The boats run on tracks, I think. They don't really float."

Stacey smiled at me. "Thanks, Byron," she said. "I'm feeling better already."

Pirates of the Caribbean is a cool ride. You tour around in these dark cavelike tunnels and watch these scenes that move. They show a band of really good pirates (eyepatches, black hats, striped stockings, the works) raiding a little town in the Caribbean. You feel like you're actually there.

In one place, the pirates set some buildings on fire. The buildings really, really look like they're on fire, too — all red and yellow and glowing. In another place, you pass under a pirate sitting on a bridge or something and you can see that he has hairy legs! There are drunk pirates, there's a gunfight between two ships, with the exploding shells splashing the water all around your boat, and there are funny pirates in jail. A dog has the keys to their prison, but he won't give them up!

"Boy, some ride!" said Adam as we climbed out of our boat.

"I'll say," said Stacey. "I'm not a bit seasick. That was great."

We were all talking and asking questions as we walked outside.

"How did they make that fire?" asked Nicky. "Was it real?"

"What about that gunfight?" said Jordan.

"I liked the drunk pirates," said David Michael. "Yo ho ho and a bottle of rum!"

Jordan began to get silly. David Michael's song had reminded him of another one. "How dry I am," he sang. "How wet I'll be, if I don't find, the bathroom key!"

"Jordan," warned Stacey.

"How about this one?" I added. "Comet, it makes your mouth turn green. Comet, it tastes like Listerine. Comet, it makes you vomit. So get some Comet and vomit to —"

"Oh, wow!" Nicky suddenly cried. "Would you look where we are?"

I stopped singing. We all stopped walking. We had gotten off the ride and exited right into a gift shop. And we were surrounded by pirate stuff. There were black, three-cornered pirate hats. There were fake hooks for in case you lost your hand in a swordfight. There were necklaces with skulls on them and pirate flags and rubber daggers.

"Awesome," I said. "Totally awesome."

We all wanted to buy something. And we decided we should each buy something different so that when we got together in Stoneybrook we'd have a really good collection of pirate stuff.

It took us ages to decide what to get. Finally I bought a hat, David Michael bought a skull necklace, Jordan bought a hook, Adam bought a dagger, and Nicky bought a flag.

"You know," I said when we'd finished paying for all the stuff, "we should really hunt for
treasure now. We're all set for it. Do you guys
want to?"

"Sure!" they replied.

"And," added Nicky, "where we find treasure,
we *might* find the stowaway from the ship."

I wasn't following Nicky's thinking on that
one, but it didn't matter.

I pulled the map out of my pocket. It was more
crumpled than ever. You could still read it,
though. Then I pulled out a map of the Magic
Kingdom. "Let's see," I said. My brothers and
David Michael crowded around to look at the
maps. "We should probably search somewhere
near water, right?"

"Right," they said.

"What about Tom Sawyer's Island in
Frontierland? You have to take rafts to get over
there. And we wanted to go anyway."

"We're there!" cried Adam.

Most of us had already been to Tom Sawyer's
Island, which was why we wanted to go again. It
was almost as awesome as the pirate gift shop.
We liked firing off the air guns at the fort.

But this time we were going there to hunt for

treasure. We set to work as soon as we got off the raft.

"Should we split up or what?" asked Adam with a sly grin.

"Oh, no! No you don't! You can't fool me," said Stacey. "You guys stick together and I stick with you. Got it?"

"Got it," we said glumly.

We began our search. It wasn't as much fun as being on Treasure Cay, where we could dig up sand and turn over rocks and stuff. And where we didn't need a baby-sitter. At least — it wasn't as much fun at first.

But *then* . . . I found it! Treasure! A *real treasure*! I was crossing the floating barrel bridge and thought I saw something shiny. I leaned over and took a closer look. Something *gold* was snagged on one of the barrels. Very carefully, I picked it up. It was a bracelet and it was real old. The clasp was broken, but otherwise it looked okay. I wondered just how old it was. As old as pieces of eight? As old as a jewel from a pirate-raided town in the Caribbean?

I held it up and examined it in the sunlight. The golden links looked worn and kind of dirty.

And valuable.

"You guys! You guys!" I yelled.

The others were ahead of me. They'd reached the end of the bridge. I ran to catch up.

"I found treasure!" I shrieked.

Everyone crowded around me — even a few people I didn't know.

"Look at this bracelet," I said. "It must be as old as pirates. They could have stolen it off some poor lady when they raided a town."

It was right then that I noticed Stacey looking at me kind of strangely. "What?" I said. "What did I do wrong?"

"Nothing," she said sadly. She held out her hand. "May I see the bracelet, please, Byron?"

I handed it to her.

"I'm really sorry to say this," she went on (and she sure did sound sorry), "but this bracelet is Dawn's. She lost it yesterday. Did it have a glass charm on it shaped like a unicorn?"

"No," I replied. "Are you *sure* this is Dawn's bracelet? That's a pretty big whaddyacallit — a pretty big coincidence."

"Amazing but true," said Adam in this eerie voice.

"The charm must have slipped off," Stacey went on. "The bracelet is old, though, Byron. You were right about that. It's an antique. It belonged to Dawn's great-aunt. Dawn liked this bracelet a whole lot. She was upset when she lost it. I think it's a family heirloom or something. She'll be really grateful that you found it."

I nodded. I felt good about that. Honest I did. But not as good as if I'd found a treasure. And Nicky was disappointed that we hadn't seen the stowaway, either, although how he thought we were going to find him in the middle of Disney World was beyond me.

That night, my brothers and David Michael and I presented the bracelet to Dawn. She was so happy she cried. For a moment, I thought she was going to kiss me. (Dis*gust*.) I'm glad she didn't.

Us guys decided to quit looking for treasure at the Magic Kingdom, but somehow I just couldn't make myself throw the treasure map away. I stuck it in the back pocket of my jeans.

CHAPTER 20

Karen

I am so sad. I'm happy . . . but I'm sad. Do you know what I mean? It's that feeling you get when your birthday finally comes and you're really happy that the waiting is over. And you're going to get presents and a cake and a party. But you're also really sad that the waiting is over. Because when the day ends, your birthday will end, too. And you won't have it to look forward to anymore.

That is how I felt on our last day at Disney World. I had a million things to look forward to — but when the day was over, our trip would be almost over, too. We were all flying home the next day.

Here are the things I was most especially looking forward to:

1. One more ride on Cinderella's Golden Carousel.
2. One more ride on Dumbo, the Flying Elephant.
3. The parade. (We kept missing it. We *still* hadn't seen it.)

AND!!

4. Breakfast with the Disney characters!

I am not joking! Mommy and Daddy and Andrew and David Michael and I were going to go on a steamboat called the *Empress Lilly* and eat breakfast. And guess who was going to walk around in the dining room: Pluto and Tigger and maybe some other characters!

The breakfast began at 9:00 a.m. and Andrew and David Michael and I were just a smidge excited. Oh, all right. We were really really really really really really really excited.

When we got to the *Empress Lilly* we waited in a long line outside. A lady took our names, and another lady gave name tags to Andrew and David Michael and me. We stuck them on our shirts. I wanted a name tag for my hitchhiking ghost who was still with me, but I didn't know what his name was. So I didn't say anything. I wondered if I should, though. That ghost still made my skin creep, so I thought I should be nice to him. He hadn't done anything mean to me yet, though. He was just hanging around.

After lots and lots and lots of waiting, the line began to move and we walked toward the *Empress Lilly*. It was a beautiful white boat with a big paddle wheel.

"Daddy, where are we going to go?" I asked. I was looking beyond the boat to the water.

Daddy cleared his throat. There are only three times he does that: 1) When his throat is tickly. 2) When he's embarrassed about something. 3) When he has to tell us something he knows we won't like to hear.

"Well," he began, "we're not going to go anywhere. The *Empress Lilly* is just for show. It's not a working boat."

"Really?" I said. I felt disappointed. And I hoped my ghost wouldn't be mad. Maybe he'd been looking forward to a boat ride.

"Yes," Daddy told me. "But still, you get to go on board a paddle wheeler. And you get to see Pluto."

"Right! Oh, Daddy, if Pluto comes to our table, you'll take his picture, won't you?"

"Of course," said Daddy.

We filed onto the boat and a waiter showed us

into a dining room. He pointed to a table with five seats, and Daddy and Elizabeth and my brothers and I sat down. A basket of donut holes was in the middle of the table. Andrew and David Michael and I all pounced on the chocolate donuts. We left the cinnamon ones for Daddy and Elizabeth.

The room was very nice, but it looked like any old dining room. You'd never have known we were on a steamboat, except that you could see water out the window. I didn't have much time to think about that, though. As soon as the tables were filled up, a man strode into the middle of the room. He welcomed us to the breakfast. Then he asked if anybody was having a birthday.

"I am!" called a boy.

"Well, that's wonderful," said the man. He walked over to the boy and looked at his name tag. "Tomás," he said. "And how old are you today?"

"Eight."

"Let's all sing 'Happy Birthday' to Tomás."

The man raised his arms and began to sing. Everyone joined in. The grown-ups smiled at him. The kids looked at him like he was really special. Boy, what a lucky duck, I thought.

When the song was over, the man said, "Any other birthdays?"

I couldn't help it. I stood up. "Me!" I called. "It's my birthday!"

I have always wanted a whole dining room full of people to sing to me and smile at me and look at me like I'm special.

"Karen!" my father whispered loudly. "It's not —"

Too late. The man had come over to our table.

"Another birthday!" he exclaimed. "Two in one day. That doesn't happen very often."

Daddy and Elizabeth smiled nervously.

"How old are you?" the man asked me.

"Seven," I told him.

David Michael snorted. It was really rude of him.

But the man didn't seem to notice. He just looked at my tag and announced that my name was Karen. Then everyone began to sing again.

I beamed. I loved it. I loved being right in the middle of things, with everyone thinking about *me*. I didn't care that it wasn't my birthday. It was probably my only chance ever to have about a hundred people sing to me.

The song ended. While the singing had been going on, the waiters had been busy serving up plates of bacon, scrambled eggs, and potatoes. I looked down at my food. Then I lifted my fork.

"Karen," my father said in a low voice. "Don't you ever do that again, young lady. You told a lie."

"I know. I'm sorry."

"I have half a mind to make you wait outside with me until breakfast is over."

"Oh, no! Please, Daddy."

"But I'm not going to. Not here. Not on the last day of our vacation. Besides, everyone thinks it's your birthday."

"I know," I said. I squirmed uncomfortably. I hate making Daddy mad. "I just wanted everyone to sing to me. Besides, my ghost made me do it. My hitchhiking ghost. He's with me all the time." Right away I wished I hadn't said that. I knew it wasn't true. He hadn't made me do it. Would I make the ghost mad? I waited for something to happen. Nothing did.

Nothing ghostly, anyway.

But David Michael scowled at me from across the table. "You are such a baby," he said.

"I am not."

"Are too." He began to sing, "Kindergarten baby, stick your head in gravy. Wash it off with —"

But Daddy stopped him.

"David Michael. Karen. That is enough. Both of you."

David Michael didn't finish the song. But when Daddy and Elizabeth weren't looking, he stuck his tongue out at me. I stuck mine back out at him.

Then, from across the room, I heard a cheer. Andrew and David Michael and I craned our necks to see what was going on. Tigger the tiger from *Winnie-the-Pooh* had bounced into the room!

"Oh, it's Tigger!" I exclaimed.

Tigger began walking from table to table. Nearly everyone wanted to take his picture. While that was happening, someone began handing out comic books to all the kids. The comics were about Epcot Center, and they were called "Mickey and Goofy Explore the Universe of Energy." Stuck in each book was a yellow *Empress Lilly* pennant.

I saw a kid ask Tigger to sign his pennant. So when Tigger finally got to our table, I handed him my pennant and a pen. Tigger signed his name!

"Thank you!" I cried.

After awhile Tigger left the room. I looked down at my food. I was much too excited to eat. Andrew and David Michael were too excited, too.

"Eat up, kids," said Elizabeth. But just then, Pluto came in.

"Yay!" I cheered. Pluto walked from table to table with his long red tongue hanging out. Daddy snapped a picture of Pluto with his arms around my brothers and me.

Soon it was time to leave.

"Can't any of you kids eat even one more bite?" asked Elizabeth.

David Michael and Andrew and I shook our heads.

So we got on a bus and headed back to the Magic Kingdom one last time.

"What shall we do first?" asked Elizabeth as we walked down Main Street.

"The carousel?" I said. "Could we ride on the carousel?"

Elizabeth looked at my brothers. "Is that okay with you guys?"

"Sure," said Andrew.

David Michael shrugged. He was still mad because all those people had sung "Happy Birthday" to me and thought I was seven.

We walked toward Fantasyland. Andrew said he had to go to the bathroom.

"I'll take him," said Daddy. "We'll meet you at the carousel."

"Okay," replied Elizabeth. "Hey, David Michael! Don't wander off. Come back!" Elizabeth ran after David Michael.

My socks were falling down. I stopped and pulled them up. When I looked around, I couldn't see Elizabeth or David Michael or Daddy or Andrew.

"Elizabeth?" I called.

I was in a big crowd of people.

"Elizabeth? . . . ELIZABETH!"

"Are you lost, little girl?" asked a popcorn vendor.

Even though I hate being called "little girl," I said, "Yes." I wanted to cry. But do you know what? I wasn't really *too* scared. My ghost was with me, and suddenly I imagined that he was a friendly ghost instead of a scary one. After all, he hadn't done anything mean to me, and besides, he was the only person I knew here. I imagined him saying, "Don't worry. We'll find Elizabeth and your daddy." And I felt better!

The popcorn vendor asked someone who worked in a store to sell his popcorn for him for awhile. Then he began asking me all sorts of questions, like where was I supposed to meet Elizabeth, and which bathroom did I think Daddy had taken Andrew to?

I tried to answer him as he walked me to the carousel.

"What's your stepmother wearing?" he wanted to know.

"A pink dress, I think." But I wasn't sure. I'd been so excited about breakfast that I hadn't paid much attention.

"Well, we'll look for pink dresses," said the man pleasantly.

He reached out his hand. I held onto him with my left hand — and onto my hitchhiking ghost with my right hand.

"Is that your stepmother?" the popcorn vendor wanted to know. He was pointing to a fat woman in a pink sundress.

I shook my head. "No."

We kept walking.

"What if Elizabeth isn't at the carousel?" I asked. My voice was trembling.

"Then we'll look for your daddy. He's supposed to go to the carousel, too. Don't worry. I've worked at the Magic Kingdom for three years and I've seen lots of lost kids. Don't you worry about a thing. I never got one whose parents I couldn't find. It always works out. Trust me."

"Always?" I asked. (My ghost squeezed my hand.)

"Always."

When we reached the carousel, guess what we saw first thing?

Elizabeth!

"There she is!" I cried. (She was wearing blue jeans and a yellow shirt.)

"Where?" asked the popcorn vendor. (I guess he was looking for a pink dress.)

"There." I ran to Elizabeth and threw my arms around her.

"Oh, thank heavens," she said. "I was hoping you'd find your way here."

We hugged a long time. Then Elizabeth thanked the popcorn vendor.

And I thought about my new secret: My hitchhiking ghost really was friendly. He wasn't scary. I decided I wanted him to come back to Stoneybrook with me. Maybe he could get to know old Ben Brewer, the ghost of the third floor at Daddy's house.

CHAPTER 21

Stacey

It was our last day at Disney World, and guess where I was going to spend it — at Epcot Center. (By the way, in case you're wondering, Epcot stands for Experimental Prototype Community of Tomorrow. I have no idea what that means. Maybe I will after I look up "prototype," but I'm not going to bother with that until I get back to Stoneybrook.) Anyway, Claire and Margo wanted to go. They were the only Pike kids who did. The others preferred the Magic Kingdom. So I volunteered to take them. I was pretty curious about Epcot myself.

As usual, after breakfast we boarded a bus outside the hotel. This one took us to Epcot. Claire and Margo were excited. After two days at the Magic Kingdom they'd done everything they wanted to do. Now they were ready for something new.

While we were on the bus, we looked at a pamphlet about Epcot Center.

"Which is the ride with the dinosaurs?" Margo wanted to know. "My friend Betsy said that's the funnest."

"Let's see," I said. I began leafing through the pamphlet.

While I was looking, Claire spoke up. "What *is* Epcot, anyway?"

I tried not to smile. Why had Claire wanted to go to Epcot Center so badly if she didn't know what it was? "What's Epcot?" I repeated.

"No," said Margo. "Which is the dinosaur ride?"

"Whoa!" I exclaimed. "One question at a time. Okay. Margo, the dinosaurs are in the Universe of Energy. We'll try to go there first. Now, Claire. Let me see, Epcot is a place where we can learn about our world and about the future."

Claire frowned. "That sounds like . . . like . . ."

"School," supplied Margo.

"But it won't be," I said. "I promise. It'll be fun. In school do you get to ride through a land filled with dinosaurs?"

"No," replied both girls.

"Do you get to see a new, really cool *three-D* video starring Michael Jackson?"

"No," said Claire.

"Three-D?!" cried Margo. "You mean we wear those funny glasses?"

"Yup."

"All right!"

"And what else?" asked Claire. "What else is there?"

We looked through the pamphlet together. There was Journey Into Imagination, which sounded like a lot of fun. And World of Motion and Spaceship Earth. Then there was the World Showcase, with food and souvenirs from eleven different countries.

"Oh, boy!" said Claire. "Pretty exciting."

But as far as the girls were concerned, the most exciting thing happened just as we were walking toward the *geosphere* (that's what it's called) that stands at the entrance to Epcot Center. It looks like a gigantic golf ball, and inside it is the Spaceship Earth ride. Anyway, we were walking toward it, and suddenly Claire let go of my hand and began running away from us.

"Claire!" I shouted. "Come back!"

But she didn't hear me. She was calling, "Marc! Marc!"

"Hey, look!" exclaimed Margo. "It's Marc Kubacki and his parents."

Sure enough, Claire ran straight to the Kubackis. She greeted Marc exuberantly. Then she looked back at us. "Stacey!" she called. "Come here!"

Margo and I were already on our way. When we reached the Kubackis, there were hellos all around. Margo and Marc grinned at each other, and I shook hands with Marc's parents.

"We just got here," Claire announced.

"So did we," replied Marc. "Are you going to stay all day?"

"Almost all day," I informed him. "We're going to try to get back to the Magic Kingdom in time for the parade and the fireworks. We keep missing them, so tonight's our last chance."

"Same here!" said Marc. "We're going to go to the parade, too. Hey, Mom," he said. "I have to ask you something."

Mrs. Kubacki leaned over and Marc whispered in her ear. Then, "Sure," we heard her say. "If they want to."

Marc looked at Claire and Margo and me. "Do you guys want to come with us today?" he asked. "We could go around together. Guess what — I can go on every ride here. There isn't a single one that's too wild."

"Can we, Stacey?" Margo asked me.

"Of course," I replied. "That would be great."

And that was the beginning of one of the most interesting, surprising, and eventually sad days of my life. The interesting and surprising parts were the rides and exhibits. It was also pretty interesting to find out how accessible Epcot Center was for a wheelchair user. I'd seen plenty of kids in wheelchairs at the Magic Kingdom. And I'd seen people carefully putting them on some of the easy rides, like Peter Pan's Flight. But I hadn't paid much attention, I guess. Now, spending a day with Marc, I paid a lot of attention. Not only was everyone nice to him (not gooey-sweet nice, just regular-kid nice), but they acted as if a person in a wheelchair wasn't at all unusual and certainly wasn't any trouble. At most places, an attendant would see us and say something like, "And how many are in this party?"

One of us would reply, "Six," and then they'd give us any help we needed. It was all so easy and pleasant and natural.

The very first place we went was the Universe of Energy. It turned out that Marc was just as crazy about dinosaurs as Claire and Margo were.

"I know all about dinosaurs," he said as we

waited in line. "Tyrannosaurus rex, stegosaurus, brontosaurus, allosaurus —"

"And the birds were called dactyls," Claire interrupted.

"Pterodactyls," Margo informed her.

When we were finally inside, we were shown into a "traveling theater" with huge long seats that are more like train cars. We sat on a special one at the back that was designed to have enough room for Marc's wheelchair. The lights went out, just like in a regular movie house, and we watched films about energy and the long-ago times in which fossils were created.

And *then* our seats began to move! They turned around until they'd formed a sort of train, and we rode right out of the theater — and into a primeval forest. Soon we were in dino-saur land.

The kids were beside themselves as we rode through the darkness with the moving dinosaurs towering over us.

"Look!" Margo exclaimed. "It's a bronto-saurus!"

"Hey, there's an allosaurus and a stegosaurus having a fight!" said Marc, awed.

Nothing impressed them more than that fight.

194

It was all they talked about as we waited on line for the World of Motion.

After the World of Motion, they were laughing so hard that the Kubackis had to warn Marc to calm down.

"But did you see those accident scenes?" he said. "The bike accident? And the car accident with the boxes of fruit knocked all over the street?"

The World of Motion is about transportation, and the kids loved it (although not as much as they loved the dinosaurs). The ride was a lot of fun, and practically every scene made them giggle.

After the World of Motion we went to the Magic Eye Theater at Journey Into Imagination and saw the Michael Jackson video "Captain EO." The kids thought it was funny, exciting, and deliciously scary.

When the video was over, the Kubackis said that Marc needed some time to rest and take his medicine, so we went to a restaurant in the World Showcase for lunch. The little outdoor tables there were so small that we let the girls and Marc sit at one, while I sat at another with the Kubackis.

That was when the sad thing happened.

The kids were chattering away and I said something to the Kubackis like, "It looks as if Marc is having the time of his life."

"We hope so," replied Mrs. Kubacki. And she kind of choked on her words.

"What's the matter?" I whispered, suddenly feeling afraid.

The Kubackis glanced at each other. There was an embarrassing silence. Then Mr. Kubacki said in a low voice, "Marc is going to have major surgery in a couple of weeks. Heart surgery. It'll be very risky."

I figured out what he *wasn't* saying: that Marc might not survive the operation. I was stunned. "Does he know?" I managed to ask.

"He knows about the surgery," replied Mr. Kubacki, "but not the risks. There's no need for him to know that. We took this vacation together . . . just in case. And we want him to be happy. If . . . anything happens, this is one of the good times Mrs. Kubacki and I will be able to look back on." Mr. Kubacki reached for his wife's hand.

I swallowed hard. I couldn't let myself cry. Not there. Not then.

I saved it for late that night when Marc's last

day at Disney World was over. I lay in the darkness wondering why it was that some people are given health, and others are given trials or tests. And why such a little boy as Marc had to be given such a big test.

CHAPTER 22

Claudia

"Here they come! Here they come!" called Karen Brewer.

She meant Mickey and Minnie Mouse.

The parade was moving down Main Street in the Magic Kingdom and we were finally there to see it.

When I say "we," boy, do I mean *we*! Everyone was there: Kristy and her family, the Pikes, and all us baby-sitters. Plus, I was standing with Timothy, Dawn was with Parker and two little boys, the youngest Pike girls were with Marc Kubacki and his parents, and Kristy had brought along Mr. Staples. I thought I'd even seen Alexandra, that weird friend of Mary Anne's, hanging around. All the kids were in front, right on the curb for the best view of the parade, and the rest of us were standing behind them. The only person who could have made the group more complete was my Secret Admirer. Since we'd been at Disney World he'd left a stuffed animal at the door to our room, and sent me some barrettes and a note saying I was "as beautiful as ever" — but he hadn't shown his face.

I couldn't dwell on him, though. Not when I was holding Timothy's hand and feeling grown-up.

"Some parade, huh?" Timothy said to me.

"I'll say," I agreed.

A gigantic upside-down birthday cake with the candles stuck in the bottom (or the top) went by and Claire, Margo, Karen, and Andrew burst into giggles.

A jolly, laughing Winnie-the-Pooh went by and waved to Marc Kubacki. It was Marc's turn to giggle. What a great sight.

So why did Stacey suddenly look like she was about to cry? Her face crumpled up — just for a second. Then she made an effort to control herself. What was going on? I'd have to ask her about that later.

Alice in Wonderland skipped down the street and I watched her blow a kiss to Karen Brewer.

"Hey, Tim! Tim!" someone called from behind me.

Karen pretended to catch the kiss and blow it back.

"*Tim!*" the voice called more insistently. "Timothy!"

I turned around. Did the person the voice belonged to mean *my* Timothy?

I nudged him. "I think someone's calling you," I said.

Timothy had turned bright red. "Naw," was all he said.

But at that moment a hand clapped down on his shoulder. "*Timothy!* Hey, little brother, are you in outer space?"

It was that weird girl, Alexandra Carmody.

"Little brother! You're Timothy's sister?" I asked the girl.

"Unfortunately."

"How come you didn't tell me you had a sister?" I exclaimed, turning to Timothy.

Timothy opened his mouth, but before any words escaped, Alexandra said, "There's probably a lot you don't know about Timothy."

I couldn't help it: I took the bait. "Like what?" I asked.

"Like who our parents are," said the girl.

"Oh, yeah. Well, I guess they'd be Viv and Vernon Carmody," I said slowly. (Mary Anne had told me everything about Alex. But neither of us had realized that Alex's brother was *Timothy*.)

The girl raised her eyebrows. "So you've talked to her already, Timothy. Good for you. And see? She still likes you." Alexandra looked at me. "I *told* Tim he'd have to confess about the Secret Admirer stuff before the trip ended. It was only fair," she added.

"You're Timothy's sister?" exclaimed another voice.

Mary Anne was at my elbow. My head was spinning. The parade was marching by and we were all missing it.

"Well, I *tried* to tell you that," Alexandra said indignantly to Mary Anne. "But you wouldn't let me."

I looked from Mary Anne to Alexandra to Timothy with my mouth open. (Timothy just kept staring at the ground.)

"You mean you were going to tell me the truth?" Mary Anne said to Alexandra.

"Yes."

Mary Anne paused. Then, "Why do you lie so much?" she asked.

"To get attention," Alexandra replied matter-of-factly. "And to make life a little more interesting.

For the same reasons Timothy spies on people and hides in coiled-up rope and stuff. Makes things interesting. When you're the children of Viv and Vernon Carmody, you tend to get lost in the shuffle. You have to find ways to . . . to . . ."

Mary Anne was frowning. "But how come you didn't just tell the *truth*?" she interrupted. "It's certainly as interesting as your lies."

Alexandra looked puzzled. "I don't know," she said at last.

"Well, tell me the truth about one more thing," Mary Anne went on. "No, two more things."

"Okay."

"*Do* you know Spider?"

"Yes. I was telling the truth the first time."

"And he's not on this trip?"

"No way."

"Ooh," said Mary Anne. "Wait'll I get my hands on Mallory. I thought it was weird that no one ever saw Spider after she did." Then she looked at Alexandra, and Alexandra looked at Mary Anne, and they burst out laughing. It looked like Mary Anne was going to forgive her after all.

I turned my attention away from the hyenas. During their entire conversation I'd kept hearing Alexandra's words: "I *told* Tim he'd have to confess about the Secret Admirer stuff. . . ."

I put my hand on Timothy's arm. "What Secret Admirer stuff?" I asked gently.

Timothy shook his head. "I was going to tell you," he said. "I really was. Honest. After the parade or something. . . ." His voice trailed off.

"You're my Secret Admirer?"

Timothy nodded.

"So why did you let me think you weren't?"

"Because . . . I don't know. In case you thought the Secret Admirer thing was dumb, I guess."

I wasn't sure what to say.

"I mean," Timothy rushed on, "I found out pretty quickly that you really liked the idea of the Secret Admirer. But by then it was too late. I'd already made up that story about seeing a redheaded guy run by." He paused. "Are you mad?"

"No," I answered quickly. "I'm . . ." What was I? I had to admit that I was a little disappointed. My Secret Admirer wasn't Spider, (although I hadn't *really* thought he might be). He wasn't a mysterious foreigner or a lonely prince. He wasn't even secret anymore. Furthermore, Timothy had lied to me. His lying was different from his sister's, since he'd done it with good intentions, and probably because he was shy. Still, he had lied.

I felt fooled.

"I feel fooled," I told him.

Timothy put his arm around me. "I'm *really* sorry," he said. "Remember that first day we met, when you were trying to figure out why your admirer wanted to be secret, and I suggested it was because he was afraid you wouldn't like him?"

"Yes."

"Well, I was talking about me, of course."

"How could you think anyone wouldn't like you?" I asked.

Timothy smiled. "That's exactly what I needed to hear," he said. "So you're not mad?"

"To quote you," I replied, "naw. . . . Hey, what's all this about spying on people and hiding in coiled-up rope?"

Timothy grinned. "Have you ever tried it? Spying, I mean? It's great. You'd be amazed what you can find out. You just have to be agile — and ready to run if you think you're going to get caught."

I burst out laughing. "So you've been hiding in places and running away? The Pike kids thought there was a stowaway on the *Ocean Princess*. They must have seen you!"

Timothy laughed. "I don't believe it!"

"Oh, no," I said. "Guess what. We just missed the whole parade." The last float was disappearing down the street. The people around us were wandering away.

"But we didn't miss the fireworks," Timothy replied. We walked around the park for awhile. At 10:00 the sky suddenly exploded into showers of pink and yellow and blue and green sparks.

Timothy and I watched in silence. When the last boom had sounded, Timothy cupped my face in his hands and gently kissed my lips.

Kristy called a late meeting of the Baby-sitters Club that night. "Just a short one," she said on the way back to the hotel. "We're all tired. But we need to have one more meeting before the trip is over."

What a meeting it was. Stacey told us about Marc Kubacki, and Mary Anne burst into tears. When she'd calmed down, Mary Anne told the others about Alexandra, and I told them about Timothy.

"But," Mary Anne finished up, "I don't think I'll keep in touch with Alex. We could never be friends. She lies for the sake of lying. How could I trust her?"

I didn't feel that way about Timothy at all, but I didn't have to say a thing. Everyone had seen us together. And I knew I'd remember his kiss for the rest of my life. The only thing that could have made that moment better was a photo — a picture of us that I could look at whenever —

Wait a sec!

"You guys!" I cried. "I've got it! I've got it!"

"What?" shrieked my friends.

"I know what to give the Brewers and the Pikes!"

"What?" they shrieked again.

"We'll put together albums full of photos of the trip and of their kids. We've all been taking pictures. I bet we've got tons of great shots. We can organize the albums to show everything from boarding the *Ocean Princess* to our last day here at Disney World. And then we can write about the trip. A sort of diary to go with the pictures."

Everyone began exclaiming things like, "Fantastic!" and "Super idea!"

And Kristy said, "Now *that's* meaningful."

Then we started trying to remember just what pictures we had taken. The list was long. And good. Karen Brewer with her manicure, the boys looking for treasure. Stacey thought she'd gotten one of Claire and Margo with Marc Kubacki.

"Okay," said Kristy. "So what we do when we get home is have our film developed right away, and buy two nice albums, and some notebooks to write in. We can pay for everything with money from the club treasury. Then we'll ask the other kids to help us. This meeting is adjourned."

CHAPTER 23

Kristy

Our trip is over. I can't believe it. We got up early this morning, packed, ate a very fast breakfast in the coffee shop, and then everyone who was on the trip waited outside the hotel. It was a sea of people and luggage.

Buses started arriving. Most of us were going to the Orlando airport to catch flights home. What a mob scene.

The airport was even worse because we all wanted to say our good-byes. Of course, my family and friends and the Pikes were flying home on the same plane. But we had new friends to say good-bye to.

I saw Dawn and Parker, and Claudia and her "Secret Admirer," trying to say private farewells. It wasn't easy. The airport was crowded. They must have felt like fish in a bowl with everyone watching them.

I saw Stacey with the Kubackis. First she spoke to Mr. and Mrs. Kubacki. After a few minutes, both she and Marc's mother opened up their purses and took out pens and pads of paper. They were probably exchanging addresses. Then they put their things away, and Stacey leaned over to talk to Marc. After a moment, he wrapped his skinny arms around her neck in a tight hug. Stacey gave him a kiss good-bye. As she straightened up, I could see that she was struggling not to cry.

Not too far away, Mary Anne was talking to Alexandra Carmody. They exchanged addresses, too, but I knew Mary Anne would never write to her.

I felt a tap on my shoulder and turned around. Mr. Staples was standing behind me.

I grinned at him.

"Well," he said, "guess this is it."

"I guess so."

"You know, I've got six grandchildren. All boys. Great kids. But if I had a granddaughter, I'd want one just like you."

"Thanks," I replied in a voice barely above a

whisper. "And if one of my grandfathers were alive, I'd hope he was just like *you*."

"Well . . . hmphh," said Mr. Staples, but I could tell he was pleased.

"Hey," I went on, "there's always Nannie. You two should really get acquainted."

"Don't know about that. I'm not much on long-distance relationships. How does your nannie feel about Arizona?"

"I have no idea," I said. "Can I give her your phone number and address?"

"Do you have them?"

"No, but I want them — so *we* can write to each other. And so I can maybe call you from time to time. Watson would let me, I think. You could tell me about your grandsons."

Mr. Staples looked thoughtful. "Zach is just your age," he said.

"Really? Where does he live?"

"Seattle."

"Oh. I'm not big on long-distance relationships myself. But you and I — we could be pen pals or phone pals. Couldn't we?"

" 'Course we could."

"Great." I opened my knapsack and found some paper and a pen. I'd bought the pen at the Magic Kingdom. On the cap was a picture of Mickey Mouse dressed as the Sorcerer's Apprentice.

I scribbled out my address and phone number and gave the slip of paper to Mr. Staples. He folded it in half very carefully and stuck it in his shirt pocket behind a couple of pens.

"Now you," I said.

Mr. Staples dictated his address and phone number to me.

"I'm warning you," I said. "As soon as we get to Stoneybrook, I'm going to make a copy of this for Nannie." I waved the paper at Mr. Staples.

He smiled sadly at me. "You're one in a million, kiddo," he said gruffly.

"Aw, come on."

"Attention, please!" A tinny voice filled the air. "Now boarding Flight Three Sixteen to Tucson, Flight Three Sixteen to Tucson."

"Well, that's me," said Mr. Staples.

Suddenly I didn't know what to say.

I don't think Mr. Staples did, either. At last he just held his arms out. I gave him a big hug around his waist. Afterward, Mr. Staples had to blow his nose three times before he could pick up his suitcase. When he was ready, he waved to me. I waved back.

Then he walked away.

I looked down at the paper with his address on it. A tear dripped off the end of my nose and landed on the paper. It splotched up the ink.

"What a dope you are," I scolded myself. I blotted the tear away.

"Kristy! Kristy! Come on!"

It was Karen.

I turned around. Our group was getting ready to find our gate. There were twenty minutes until take-off. I ran after Karen.

We boarded the plane like old pros. It looked just like the other plane, with two seats, an aisle, five seats, another aisle, then two more seats in each row. This time, I sat in the middle of the five seats. Karen and Andrew sat on one side of me, Dawn and Claudia on the other. In front of us were the triplets, Nicky, and David Michael. They had all their pirate stuff out. I hoped they weren't going to be too noisy.

We buckled our seat belts. Then we put our seat backs and trays in an upright position.

The plane began taxiing down the runway.

"Lift-off!" I heard David Michael cry as we nosed into the air.

Across the aisle, Margo Pike reached for her barf bag and threw up.

"Gross-out!" shrieked the triplets.

"Oh, disgusting," added Nicky. "Margo barfs at *any*thing."

"Comet, it makes your mouth turn green," sang Jordan.

"Comet," the other boys joined in, "it tastes like Listerine. Comet, it makes you VOMIT," (five heads turned toward poor Margo), "so get some Comet and VOMIT today."

"You guys," said Mary Anne, as she handed a Kleenex to Margo. *"Can it!"*

"Can it what?" I heard Byron whisper to Adam. Luckily, Mary Anne didn't hear him.

"Kristy?" said Karen. "Is Margo sick again?"

"Yes —"

"Can I go watch?"

"Karen! Of course not." I was getting a headache.

In front of me, the boys calmed down. Dawn and Claudia and I tried to think of great pictures we'd taken that we could include in the photo albums. After quite a while, I realized that the five boys were awfully quiet. Too quiet. I tried to peek between the seats to see what they were up to. They were all peering at a little crumply piece of paper that Byron was holding. I could see some words on it in a foreign language.

And at that moment a man who was walking

down the aisle leaned way over, across Adam and Nicky, to let a flight attendant rush by him. He happened to see the crumply piece of paper.

"Pardon me," he said with an accent.

The boys looked up at him.

"You are from the Netherlands, yes?" said the man.

All five boys shook their heads.

"American?" asked the man in surprise.

"Yup," said Adam.

"Oh. My mistake. I saw the copy machine diagram. With words in Dutch. I think you are from the Netherlands, too. I am Dutch."

"Copy machine diagram?" repeated Byron. "Dutch?"

"Yes," said the man. He pointed to the paper. "My company, it manufactures copiers. That is picture of — how do you say? — the insides of a machine."

"Oh, brother," muttered David Michael as the man went on his way.

"What was that all about?" I asked Claudia and Dawn.

They shrugged.

The rest of the flight was pretty quiet.

We landed on time and Margo barfed again.

"Well," I said to Mom and Watson as we filed slowly off the plane, "it's over. I can't believe it. Back to boring old life."

Mom laughed. "Not quite yet," she said. We had entered the waiting area and she pointed straight ahead.

At first all I could see was a gigantic WELCOME HOME sign. Then I began to recognize faces: Dawn's mother and brother; Mary Anne's dad; Claudia's parents, her sister, and her grandmother, Mimi; Stacey's parents; and last but not least — Nannie.

"Nannie!" I cried. I broke away from my family and ran to her. I threw my arms around her. "Oh, Nannie! It was the most wonderful trip. You won't believe everything that happened! And guess what. I've got a boyfriend for you!"

Nannie linked her arm through mine. "Tell, tell," she said eagerly. "The trip, this boyfriend, everything."

And I began to tell her the story of our trip.

CHAPTER 24

Kristy

Two months after our trip was over, Stacey received this card in the mail:

Saturday

Dear Stacey,

It's been a long time since we said good-bye at the airport. I hope you haven't been too worried. We wanted to wait until we had definite news before we wrote to you.

Marc's surgery was difficult. He was very brave, but he kept suffering infections after the operation. The doctors had warned us about that. Still, Mr. Kubacki and I weren't prepared for how frightening it would be.

Happily, Marc was allowed to come home a week ago. His recovery is expected to be slow but steady — and complete. By this time next year, he should be a healthy, active boy. He wants a bicycle for his birthday!

Please drop us a line when you have time.

All the best
The
Kubackis

Marc wants to add something here:

P.s. Hi! I'm home! No more wheel-chair! A bike isn't the only thing I whant for my birthday. I whant a skatebord too. And I whant a back pack. To go camping. I whant to see you. Mabe we can visit Coneticut. I love you!
Love
Marc Kubacki

And that is the end of our trip. The *very* end. Stacey insisted it wasn't over until we knew how Marc's operation turned out. So now we know — successful and happy and wonderful.

Thank you, everyone, for the trip. It was the greatest trip we could imagine. And you are the greatest parents and friends we could imagine.

About the Author

Ann M. Martin's The Baby-sitters Club has sold over 190 million copies and inspired a generation of young readers. Her novels include the Newbery Honor Book *A Corner of the Universe*, *A Dog's Life*, and the Main Street series. She lives in upstate New York.

Keep reading for a sneak peek at the next
Baby-sitters Club Super Special!

Baby-sitters' Summer Vacation

"Attention, campers and counselors. Attention, campers and counselors. Please assemble for cabin assignments."

We were in the middle of our Baby-sitters Club reunion, and Charlotte Johanssen was crying all over Stacey (while I, Claudia, wanted to hug her), and then that voice came over the loudspeaker.

"What are cabin assignments?" asked Charlotte

as she pulled away from Stacey. She wiped her sleeve across her eyes and sniffled. Mary Anne handed her a Kleenex.

"That's when everyone finds out which cabin they'll be staying in while they're here," said Dawn knowingly. "We'll probably group together now — counselors, campers, and CITs."

"And junior CITs," added Mallory.

"And junior CITs," Dawn repeated.

Mallory and Jessi had been made junior CITs. It's a long story.

"Oh, I hope I'm in Becca's cabin," said Charlotte anxiously.

That announcement practically caused a riot as everyone rushed for this big open area around a flagpole, where the head of the camp was going to organize us girls. Since it looked like the organizing might take awhile, Stacey and I hung back from the rest of our friends for a few minutes.

I threw my arms around her. "It's so good to see you!" I exclaimed. "You look fabulous! What did you do to your hair?" I pulled away and held her at arm's length the way this one aunt of mine always does to me.

"Body wave," Stacey replied. "I swore up and down that I wouldn't perm it again, and then it grew out and looked funny — kind of lank. And orange-ish instead of blonde. So I settled on getting a body wave. In fact, Mom *told* me to get a body wave."

"Your own *mother*?" Unheard of.

Stacey nodded.

"Well, I think you did the right thing."

"Thanks. How are you? How's Mimi?"

"I'm fine. Mimi's okay," I replied. "Not great, but okay. It's funny. You know all the physical therapy she's been getting since she had the stroke?"

"Yup," said Stacey. And we hurried a little to start catching up with everyone.

"Well, it seems to be helping. We keep seeing improvement. But only in her body. Not in her mind. She's mixed up her sentences and forgotten words since the stroke, but now she's saying really weird things. Like, she'll wander into my room and ask me what dress Patsy stole for the dance."

"Huh?"

"I know. What does that mean? Who's Patsy? What dance? And why *steal* a dress instead of buy one or borrow one? I don't get it."

We had joined the others and were standing at the edge of the big crowd of kids. Stacey started to say something to me — to answer my questions, maybe — when we realized that the camp director was reading off lists of names and we better pay attention to her.

I knew she was the camp director because her picture was in the camp brochure. In a lot of places. Her husband is the director of the boys' side of the camp, across Lake Dekadonka or whatever it's called. Her name is Mrs. Means.

Mrs. Means. Funny.

And just as I was thinking that, I heard a girl next to me nudge her friend and say, "Old Meanie hasn't changed a bit."

Her friend giggled. "Yeah. Same as ever."

So *I* nudged Stacey and said, "Hey, Stace, they call Mrs. Means 'Old Meanie.'"

Stacey grinned.

We went back to listening to Old Meanie.

"In Meghan's cabin," she was saying, "the CITs are Sally Troner and Claudia Kishi. The campers are as follows." She rattled off a list of six campers, including Vanessa and Haley.

"Well," I said, "here goes. This is it." I looked at Stacey and at tearstained Charlotte. "I guess I'll see you later this afternoon or at supper or something."

"Bye, Claud," said Stacey nervously.

I joined a group of girls that was gathering

near Mrs. Means. "Hi," I said to the tallest one. "Are you Meghan?"

"Yup," the girl answered cheerfully.

"Good. Then this is the right group. I'm Claudia Kishi."

"Oh, our other CIT. Terrific. I think we're all here."

Gathered around me were Meghan, Vanessa, Haley, four other girls about Vanessa's age, and an older girl whom I guessed was Sally, my co-CIT. She wore her brown hair in a French braid and reminded me a little of Stacey — sophisticated, but probably not snobby. I hoped we would be friends.

"Well," said Meghan, "let's introduce ourselves, even though we'll probably forget everyone's names right away."

We laughed but agreed to try it. "I'm Meghan," Meghan began, "and I'm your counselor. We're in Cabin Nine-A, by the way, because you campers are nine years old, and we're one of the two nine-year-old groups. Isn't that an original way to name the cabins?"

More laughter. The introductions continued. The other four girls turned out to be Leeann, Brandy, Jayme, and Gail. I didn't remember their last names. I hoped I wouldn't need to.

"Okay, now comes the complicated part," said Meghan.

"Trying to repeat the names?" asked Sally.

Meghan smiled. (I definitely liked both Meghan and Sally.) "Nope," said Meghan. "Getting our luggage to Cabin Nine-A."

It really was sort of a pain. First we had to find our bags, and of course everyone else was looking for theirs, too. The first time our group thought we'd gotten all our suitcases and knapsacks together, Jayme said, "Uh-oh. Where's my Garfield bag?"

We found the Garfield bag and started up a path away from the crowd and into the woods. Then Vanessa said, "Um, Claudia? I don't think this is my suitcase."

We opened it. It wasn't.

So we had to go back. All of us.

At last, at last, at last we reached our cabin. We had walked a little way through the woods, but when I turned around to look behind me, I could still see the flagpole — the center of the camp — Old Meanie and a group of girls clustered around it.

"Here we are," announced Meghan. "Home disgusting home."

Vanessa Pike burst into giggles.

I took a good look at Cabin 9-A. It was half of a bigger cabin. Guess what the other half of the bigger cabin was called? You got it — 9-B. Another group of nine-year-olds, their counselor, and their CITs would bunk in 9-B.

Our cabin looked pretty much the way you'd imagine, especially if you've seen *The Parent Trap* and *Meatballs*. It and everything in it was wooden. The outside of the cabin was made from that rough wood — logs with the bark still on. A porch stretched across the front of 9-A and 9-B. Inside 9-A were four bunk beds for the campers and CITs, and one single bed with a curtain that could be drawn around it. That was for Meghan.

Counselors get a little privacy.

Vanessa and Haley immediately claimed a bunk for themselves. Then Sally and I took a bunk. CITs ought to stick together, we thought. Jayme and Leeann seemed to have been going to Camp Moosehead together for years, so they took the third bunk, and Gail and Brandy were left with the fourth.

When the bunks had been claimed, everyone got kind of quiet — for about five seconds. Then Meghan suggested that we unpack. There were shelves along the walls and we were supposed to put our stuff on them and stow our suitcases in the cabin's one closet.

"The room will stay neater that way," said Meghan.

So we unpacked. And we unrolled our sleeping bags on our bunks. While we did that, we began talking.

"Where do we, you know, go to the bathroom?" asked Haley, looking around the cabin suspiciously.

"The bathrooms are separate cabins," replied Jayme. "Group bathrooms."

"Ew," said Haley.

The campers started laughing.

I climbed down from my place on the top bunk to see Sally, who was below. (I stepped on her hand on the way, but she was very good-natured about it.)

"Guess what," she said, when I told her I hadn't been to Camp Moosehead before, "there's a canteen near the recreation hall where you can buy postcards and toothpaste and candy bars and things." (Junk food — yum!) "And us CITs get to have dances and stuff with the boy CITs."

Really?! Camp Moosehead was looking better every second!

Want more baby-sitting?

And many more!

Don't miss any of the books in the Baby-sitters Club series by Ann M. Martin—available as ebooks

It's fun to be a

BABY SITTERS LITTLE SISTER

Read more of Karen's adventures!

#1 Karen's Witch

#2 Karen's Roller Skates

#3 Karen's Worst Day

#4 Karen's Kittycat Club

DON'T MISS THE BABY-SITTERS LITTLE SISTER GRAPHIC NOVELS!

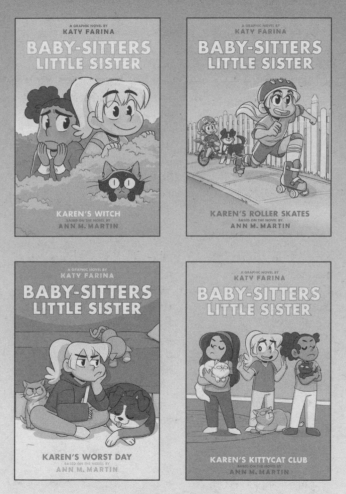

Don't miss any of the books in the Baby-sitters Little Sister series by Ann M. Martin—available as ebooks